D1525698

BLack Man's VERSION TO EXHALE

Akie Fanon Davis

Fanon Productions
Stafford, Texas

BLACK MAN'S VERSION TO EXHALE
©1998 by Akie Davis

Published by Fanon Productions

First Edition
Cover designed by PYE

Printed in the United States of America

ISBN: 0-9662369-0-4

Library of Congress Catalog Card Number: 97-095025

For information:
Fanon Productions
435 B-1 FM 1092, Suite 255
Stafford, Texas 77477

I would like to dedicate this book to my aunt, Denice, perhaps one of the strongest and positive Black women I know and who was diagnosed with breast cancer last year.

A special dedication to my fiancée, Patricia Houston. Thank you for being so supportive and understanding through the good and bad times. Thank you for restoring my faith in my beautiful Black Queens. I love you now and forever more.

ACKNOWLEDGMENTS

I would like to give a special thanks to God, for allowing me the vision to share these stories with you, because through Him all things are possible. I would also like to thank my Mom and Dad, Cain and Marie Davis, my brother Adrian Davis, and all of my family for being so supportive over the years.

A special thanks to Libby Andrews for her participation in the editing of my book. I would also like to express a special thank you to my aunts: Maxine, Jennie, Fleshia and Rosalyn for their editorial assistance and most of all for their support, prayer and encouragement throughout this project and throughout my life. Last but not least, thanks go out to my friends: Greg, Pam, Janice, Marco, Barry, Fred, Shannon and everyone else that I may have forgotten.

Contents

INTRODUCTION

Sisters Hold Your Breath While My Brothers Speak Out

We know all too well of the frustrating encounters that many Black women have had when dealing with Black men. However, little has been written on the frustration of the positive Black man in the world trying to make a relationship work. This book contains a lot of the problems and concerns that many Black men are confronted with on a daily basis. The objective of this book is to help our Black sisters realize some of the mistakes that they make in relationships and hopefully bring us closer together. It is very easy for one gender to point the finger at the other gender, but the most difficult thing for men and women to do is to self-reflect. All too often women spend countless nights going out to happy hour with their girlfriends bashing our Black men, labeling brothers and criticizing.

Over the years, I have heard so many negative things about Black men, that it has taught me how not to be. Several close female friends have also shared with me what should and should not be done on a date. I have taken negative stigmas and turned them into something positive. I have also helped many of my ex-girlfriends and friends become better people. A lot of women aren't aware of what they're doing wrong in relationships because most men don't express themselves. This book will point out some of the negative experiences that are out there from the Black man's perspective. It is up to you to figure out if you are a character in the story or if you possess any of the characteristics being portrayed.

While many sisters are literally waiting to exhale, there are countless brothers out there who are just hoping to recover. Recover from the pain, humiliation and all too often financial setback of a failed relationship at the hands (sometimes nails delicately manicured and purchased by the brother) of the beloved African Queen. My goal is that the story will not only entertain, but will cause you to self-reflect and bring you closer to Ms. or Mr. Right.

CHAPTER I

THE STORY OF KEVIN
"Rags To Moderate Riches"

Kevin is the youngest child and he has a brother named Eric who is six years older. Eric was very popular in high school. He was a good athlete, handsome, and at that time had a reputation for being a good fighter. Kevin was just the opposite. He was quiet, shy and trying to grow into a gangly body. Eric had all the women, whereas, Kevin always lived in Eric's shadow. Kevin and Eric were raised with good Christian values.

Kevin's mother had a business degree and his father was a blue-collar worker. Kevin's family lived in a middle-class neighborhood and drove a middle-class car, but didn't have a middle-class income. Kevin's parents did everything they could to keep Kevin and Eric in a prosperous environment. There were days, however, that the lights were shut off, the phone was disconnected, and Kevin went to school without lunch money. This experience proved to Kevin that he wanted to live in a nice neighborhood, but also live comfortably and within his means. Kevin took on a paper route at the age of eleven, and has been gainfully employed since that time. He learned responsibility at a very early age. He knew the value of a dollar and was good at saving money. He had big dreams of becoming a success. Kevin always had a passion for basketball, but eventually realized that he wasn't good enough to go pro. He also had dreams of running his own business. He tried just about every get-rich quick plan there was. He had owned four run-down cars by the time he became twenty-five. Women always viewed Kevin as a nice guy with no money, but a strong potential to make money. He had such high expectations for himself and soon grew tired of people saying he had potential.

Shortly after his twenty-fifth birthday, Kevin took his savings and bought a brand new shiny black BMW sports car, fully loaded. He also took some money and invested heavily into a new wardrobe. After all those years of being virtually overlooked, Kevin had finally started getting some attention, especially from women. He never dreamed that so many Black women were so materialistic. He was no longer living in the shadow of his brother. He had grown into his long, gangly body, and was actually beginning to turn quite a few heads. Kevin was now more confident than he had ever been. He actually enjoyed hearing people tell him that he was "The Man." Now all Kevin needed, he thought, was the right woman in his life to make him complete.

Enter, Hurricane
REYNA
Alias "Wreck in Effect"

Reyna is the only child. She grew up in the ghetto. Reyna has only seen her father, a pimp, approximately six times in her life. During those six encounters, she witnessed her father throw women off balconies, beat them and exploit them for money. Some people viewed Reyna as a cold-hearted bitch. She is unique in that she can relate to people in poverty because she is from the hood, but she also knows how to conduct herself in corporate America. Reyna is all about looking out for herself and her son, Jason. She won't even consider dating a man unless that man worships her. She knows then that he will sell his soul for her. She won't even consider dating a guy who just sees her as kind of cute or someone who only calls her two or three times a week.

Reyna has to get paid, and if a man offers her some cash for sex, she is down. She is cool to hang out with because she looks like a lady. She carries herself like a lady even though at times she enjoys a beer or two, listens to rap music, and plays cards with the guys. Reyna claims that she has never loved any man and never will.

She is a very cold, confident and calculating sister that feels like no woman has anything on her. She doesn't worry about the guys she dates because she feels like she is number one and that she calls all the shots. Reyna is not completely heartless though, beyond her tough lady exterior, is a compassionate soul. When she moved out of her apartment, she gave her furniture to a woman at work (that she didn't like) because the woman had children and they didn't have furniture. She also gave her last fifty dollars to a male co-worker who had cancer. Reyna would gladly give to people who were doing worst than she was, however, she is ruthless to anybody that has more than she does. She views them as being spoiled, and if they want to be with her they will have to be pre-pared to lose everything.

MICHELLE
Cash and Carry

One of Reyna's best friends is Michelle. Michelle and Reyna have been friends for about three years. They are co-workers, and often schedule a lot of activities outside of work. Michelle is married with four kids. She has had two previous marriages and only one of Michelle's children belongs to her current husband, Tom. She is only twenty-six years old and like Reyna, grew up in the hood. She doesn't love Tom, or even like him. She married Tom because he was desperately in love with her and would do any-thing for her and her kids. Michelle often comments that every time she and Tom are engaged in intimate activities, she feels like she is going to throw up.

Michelle usually sleeps with about thirteen men per year and usually keeps four men as regular sex partners. She is very straightforward and will tell you in a minute that she is all about that dollar. Michelle really thinks that she is a major money taker, but other than the way that she dresses, she doesn't have shit to show for it. She has never personally even owned a car. Her husband has a beat up little ride that is six years old. She and her husband live with Michelle's parents. Guys use to make jokes behind her back like "Tell Michelle to come turn a trick for an outfit," or "Tell Michelle to stop turning tricks to get her nails fixed."

Despite the drawbacks in her life, she was the ringleader among Reyna and their two other girl-friends for some reason. No one can quite figure out why, other than the fact that Michelle has the most clothes. They are cheap clothes at that, nothing like "Dana Buchman," "Versace," or "Donna Karan" or any other designer. Michelle probably has received the most cash and gifts from men, but she messes around with twice as many too. She has no morals, she's married and doesn't give a damn if the men she messes with are married as well. Her requirements are simple; as long as you have a couple of hundred dollars to spend on her every month, it's all good. Michelle walks around with a permanent snarl on her face, and very rarely laughs. Her friends think she is cool, but if anybody paid close attention to her, they could not help but notice that she is miserable. Michelle knows that she is getting the short end of the stick with men, but also the short end of the stick with life.

LISA
Last, (but far from least)

Reyna's other good friend is Lisa. Lisa always comes in last when it comes to conversation with the girls, over who gets what from men. Lisa is also married and has three children. She is cool, very down to earth, and has a wonderful sense of humor. Everybody likes Lisa because she isn't stuck up like her friends. Lisa actually doesn't make money an issue with the guys she dates. She is so cool and down to earth that it is hard to believe that she cheats on her husband. To Lisa, cheating is just a game that gives her a topic for conversation with her cheating girlfriends. Lisa always thought Kevin was cool. Some time ago she told Reyna how fortunate she was to have a man like Kevin. To Lisa, Kevin was everything a woman could want in a man. Lisa at times would get jealous at all the things that Kevin did for Reyna, because Lisa had never had a man do those types of things for her. She told Reyna over and over again how important it was for her to keep Kevin and to keep him happy because he was definitely a rare breed.

Lisa seemed to be very fond of her husband too. She and her husband live with Lisa's parents. She takes very good care of her kids and when it comes to clothes, of all the women, Lisa makes sure her kids have the best clothes first. Lisa really isn't concerned about how well she's dressed as much as how well her kids are dressed. Lisa is the oldest of the girls and seems to be the happiest. The girls tease her because the men she dates don't do that much for her. However, she is the type of person that finds happiness from within herself.

YOLANDA
Pleased to meet you, Mr. Rent!

Yolanda is the youngest of Reyna's good friends. She is twenty years old and has a thirty-five year old mother who has never been married. Yolanda also has a sixteen-year old sister. Part of the problem with Yolanda and many women growing up with a young mother and no father in the home is that a lot of these young mothers label the men that they date as tricks. These men aren't called by their birth names, they're called names such as rent, car note, light bill and phone bill. Most of the time these young mothers raise their daughters to do whatever they can to get money out of these men. Then it becomes a mother and daughter game about what each trick did for them that week. That's how it is in Yolanda's house, even the sixteen-year old participates in the game. Yolanda's mother Kalu didn't put any restrictions on Yolanda or her sister Carla. They were free to date whomever they wanted, when they wanted. Kalu just told them that if they were going to be hoes, just make sure that they would get paid for it. Yolanda got too deep into the game, and now has a three-year old son, and is eight months pregnant. Yolanda treated her son's father so badly that he has been missing in action for about two years. Yolanda used to tell him things like she just wanted his money and when they would fight, she would tell him that the kid was not even his son. Eventually, he got tired of Yolanda and her mother's games and walked out.

Yolanda's sister Carla has just discovered that she is two months pregnant and really isn't sure who the baby's father is. Kalu's house will eventually have three kids without any male role model around. Yolanda, despite being pregnant, is still very outgoing. She went out to the clubs with her girls up until she was six months pregnant, doing everything possible to hide her pregnancy so she could get to know new guys. Yolanda even dated a man that didn't know that she was pregnant until her fourth month. That was nothing new for Yolanda. She had a habit of convincing several guys at one time that they got her pregnant and asked each man for money to get an abortion. She would use the money to go shopping. Times used to be good for Yolanda, but now she has two children, an eight-dollar per hour job, no father around, and she is starting to lose her school-girl figure. The cute game is no longer in her favor or anyone's favor in that household.

CALVIN
"If you're Brown, I ain't down"

Kevin has a very close friend named Calvin. Calvin chooses not to date Black women because of his past experiences. He is a third year NBA player who is presently dating a white lady named Amy. Growing up, Calvin was very awkward. He was tall, lanky, with big feet and he wore glasses. Calvin never wore name brand clothes because his family was too poor. He used to get teased by the girls all the time. They would call him J.J., referring to the character on the TV show "Good Times," many years ago. When Calvin first arrived to high school, he was very aggressive, asking girls out, but nobody would go out with him. Calvin even asked this one particular girl out that he had a crush on. Calvin asked, "Why won't you go out with me?" and the woman named Monica, replied, "Because you're ugly." This devastated Calvin. He knew girls would say negative things about him in groups or behind his back, but he never thought someone would be so cruel in a one-on-one situation. This came from a girl that Calvin thought was his friend, whom he worshiped. It was at this point, that Calvin made a decision. You see, he had already asked out every available girl in the school. The girls didn't respect Calvin and they didn't respect his family because they were poor. Despite his sad situation, Calvin was a very responsible man. He was also a very hard working and determined individual. He had a good heart and would do anything within reason to help others. Calvin helped raise his younger brothers and sisters and was a chairman on the usher board at his church. He had all the necessary credentials for being a good man, other than being a little awkward and poor. Calvin's goal if he ever made anything out of himself, was to give to the underprivileged. He went ahead and dedicated himself to his studies and his basketball career. He made a promise to himself that he would dedicate his last two years of high school to becoming a better basketball player. Calvin put himself on a strenuous weight-lifting program that involved lifting weights five days a week for a minimum of two hours. He would leave the window to the school basketball gym unlocked so he could sneak in at night. Calvin began to play basketball at strange hours of the night. He played so much that the coach would run Calvin out of the gym.

Calvin would also take a bus, to the projects and play against the city's best talent. He had become a gym rat, a basketball junkie, and even put on twenty pounds of muscle. He also maintained an "A" average in all of his classes, so things began to look up for Calvin. At times he would get lonely and go back on his word and ask girls out, but the answer was still no. Calvin's senior year was great because he received a scholarship from the school of his choice. The only thing that was disappointing to Calvin was that he asked ten girls out for the prom, and all ten turned him down. He did get to go to the prom, but he went by himself. Kevin felt so bad for Calvin that he asked his date to dance with Calvin. This was the only time Calvin got to dance, but he felt bad knowing the dance was out of pity. Calvin did, however, become popular, because he was one of the team's best basketball players. The girls would talk to him; however, they wouldn't date him. Calvin decided to make one last attempt at dating a girl named Wendy. He asked her on graduation day if they could keep in touch and Wendy asked him what did he have to offer. Calvin told Wendy that with her by his side, he knew he could make it to the NBA, Wendy replied, "And if you can't?"

Calvin said that he would become an engineer. Wendy told Calvin to call her when he made it. He gave Wendy his mom's telephone number and said give me a call over the Thanksgiving and Christmas holidays. He went on to go to college and his life began to change. No longer was Calvin the frail guy everybody would make fun of. He became a sex symbol and a pro prospect. Calvin ditched the glasses and added contacts. Now he has expensive designer clothes, courtesy of his college alumni. Calvin now also owns a fully loaded Jeep Cherokee, a courtesy of the college alumni. Calvin graduated with his degree and became the 15th overall pick in the NBA draft. Now when he goes back home, he is the man. He has to fight off the sisters that wouldn't give him the time of day, back in the day. Calvin even has Monica and Wendy calling him trying to get with him, however, times have changed. He is bitter about his experiences growing up with Black women. He now dates white women, exclusively because he didn't have any contact with them until he was "Calvin the man." Feeling Calvin's pain growing up, Kevin doesn't date white women, but he understands why Calvin does. Calvin once said, "How can I be a sell-out, when my race sold me out in my time of need?" A wise man once said that people who are considered unattractive trade places with those considered attractive at least once in life.

"The Meeting of Reyna & Kevin"

It was a warm day in mid-April, when Kevin first laid eyes on Reyna. It all began with his decision to change companies. Kevin recalls the story of meeting Reyna:

"I remember going to scope out a job at this new company. I was in a strange sort of mood that day. I walked in to the reception area, and there she was, the woman of my dreams! This woman had the most beautiful skin I had ever seen. She had a light brown caramel complexion, with a smile that you only expect to see on an angel. This woman looked so pure, so clean, sexy, innocent and intelligent, all in one package. I told myself that I had to have this woman, even though she looked like the type that was taken, and probably in a monogamous relationship. To me, outside of my mother and the other women in my family, this was my first encounter with a queen. There was no limit to what I would do to make her mine. I remember asking her for an application, and she asked me if I had any experience. My knees felt so weak watching her luscious lips and pretty white teeth as her soft-spoken voice asked me questions. I told myself that if I didn't take this job, I would call back up here to ask her out. There was no way that I could ask for so much face-to-face with an angel. I immediately thought how she was the answer to all my prayers, and that she was heaven sent. When I ponder how to describe my type, not knowing for sure, she was definitely the picture of who I wanted to be with. Even though I didn't know her, I felt that I did. To make a long story short, they offered me the job, and although they didn't give me the salary that I wanted, I felt giving me the woman of my dreams was more than adequate compensation."

KEVIN'S PURSUIT OF REYNA
Can you say "Big red warning flag?"

Reyna's beauty intimidated Kevin. He was afraid to approach her to ask her out on a date, however he would make a habit of stopping by her desk several times a day to speak to her. Eventually they became friends and Kevin started buying Reyna lunch everyday at work and also buying her cards and flowers on a weekly basis. One day, Reyna asked Kevin if he would go with her to pick up her son, Jason from daycare. Kevin was delighted to go and felt that Reyna must finally feel comfortable enough with him to bring him around her son. Kevin met Jason for the first time and they immediately hit it off. Kevin took him to get something to eat and then to the park where Kevin played as if he were six years old on the monkey bars with Jason. It was getting late, so Kevin took Reyna and Jason home. He decided to go by and kick it with his cousin for a bit. They hung out, watched a ball game, drank beer and talked liked they had often done before Kevin started seeing Reyna. It was so late that Kevin just crashed on his cousin's couch for the night rather than drive all the way across town to his apartment. When Kevin got to work the next morning, Reyna called his extension and asked where he had gone the previous night because she had called him at home and got no answer. Kevin explained to her about his evening at his cousin's house but Reyna didn't believe him and hung up the telephone in the middle of his explanation. He immediately went downstairs to talk to Reyna and she told him that she was trying to get in touch with him because Jason wanted to talk to him. After a while, she got curious and called the whole night. Kevin apologized, and from that day on, Kevin was available for Reyna and Jason at their convenience. Kevin and Reyna have been together ever since.

Kevin knocked on Reyna's door early each morning. "Come on baby, we have to go to work and take the baby to school." It had become a daily routine for the two; Kevin would get the baby ready and fix him some cereal while Reyna prepared Jason's lunch. They would all leave out together like a happy little family. Kevin would walk Reyna to her desk at work, give her a kiss, tell her he loved her and give her some lunch money for the day.

The "Real" Financial Review

Michelle, Lisa, Reyna and Yolanda do lunch. Michelle asked Lisa, "what's up with Chris?" "Girl I don't know, I haven't heard from him in a week. Girl you know that I don't hear from him until he gets horny. I know one thing, I better hear from that brother before we go on our trip." Yolanda asked Reyna, "So Miss Thang, is Kevin going to give you some money to go on our trip?" "I know he will give me some money, I just don't know how much." Lisa said, "You don't know how much?" Michelle said, "I don't know how you deal with that broke ass nigga!" Reyna replied, "Let me tell you something girl, Kevin is good to me and my son. That's not his son and he takes very good care of Jason. Kevin works two jobs, goes to school, as well as to church, and he will give me his last if I asked for it. Furthermore, he treats me like a Queen." Michelle said, "Girl that sounds good, but that 'Your majesty' shit don't pay the bills. Come on, we have to go back to work."

Tony
A good man waiting to happen

Tony is Kevin's best friend and is the oldest of three kids. Tony has a brother named Steve. Tony loves the idea of being in a relationship. Having a lady or wife, is the most important thing to him. He enjoys listening to the love dedications on the radio late at night and often participates in dating games, but has yet to find Ms. Right. It seems that every time he meets someone, the relationship would never last longer than a couple of months. Tony isn't what you would call a player and he doesn't have a lot of friends. He just kind of hangs out with anybody Kevin hangs out with, and blends right in. Tony just wants to be accepted by everybody, so people, most often women, mistake his kindness to be his weakness.

Tony is just crazy about a woman that works in the building where he works. However, he hasn't got the nerve to step up to her. He thinks that this woman is everything he's dreamed about. He believes that if he could make her his lady, he would spend the rest of his life making her happy.

Tony is getting ready to move to Virginia in another week to start a business with one of his boys. Monday, Tony saw his dream lady go into Suite 500 of the K & E Law Firm; he now knew where she worked. He also knew her name was Tisha through word of mouth. Tuesday, Tony was just sitting around having a beer when he decided to call Tisha since he had some courage juice in his system. He reminded her of the couple of times they crossed paths, and she remembered him vaguely. He asked her out to lunch on Wednesday and she accepted. Tony was amazed! He thought that she was the best looking woman he had ever had an opportunity to date. Tony and Tisha went to lunch everyday for the rest of that week. She called him every afternoon after they had had lunch and told him things like she couldn't believe that she had finally met someone so nice to her and now he was leaving her. Tony couldn't believe that someone that pretty was so crazy about him.

Before Tony left for Virginia, he bought a $200 gift certificate at a local department store and put it inside of a personalized "Create-a-Card," and gave it to Tisha. As he presented the card, he said, "I don't have much but, you deserve the best." Then he gave her a hug goodbye. After Tony left town, he and Tisha wrote and called each other on a regular basis. Tisha told Tony that she wanted to come and visit him in Virginia, and he said, "Okay, I'll send you a ticket." She also told him that the job she had was through a temporary agency and she just got on permanent and found out she wouldn't be getting paid for another thirty days. Tony began to send her $100 a week to help her out until her salary kicked in. Tisha then called Tony and said she would like to move to Virginia with him, if he could provide for her and her five-year-old son. Tony told Tisha, "Baby you know I want that. You are making all my dreams come true."

During the development of his new business venture, Tony discovered that his partner was stealing money from the company's checking account and depositing it into his personal account. This had been going on since the first week Tony had been in Virginia. When he confronted his partner about the missing money, he got very defensive and told Tony that he didn't know anything about running his own business and the start-up costs that were involved. Tony decided that it would be best to just end the partnership, and pull up stakes before he suffered a major financial loss. He had also heard through the grapevine that his business partner had a $500 per day cocaine habit, which might explain the missing funds.

Tony relocated back to his hometown. He thought to himself, at least he had the courage to pursue his dreams. One day he'd try again to start his own business, but for now he could concentrate on building a life with Tisha. She told Tony that she was glad he came back home and that she wanted to marry him. Tony was ecstatic and went out and bought Tisha the biggest and brightest diamond ring that he could afford. The ring cost him $4,500.00 but he said to himself, "Nothing is too good for my lady." Tony continued to take care of Tisha even though they had yet to make love. He was a gentleman and respected Tisha for wanting to wait until after they were married.

One day Tisha called Tony and told him that she had seen a dress at Saks Fifth Avenue that she just had to have, however, she didn't have enough money. He told Tisha that she should have it and deserved it and he would bring the money up to her job before she got off work. He arrived around three thirty five, met Tisha in the lobby and handed her $175. He then said, "Well baby, I'm about to go, give me some sugar." She responded, "I don't do that." Tony was extremely hurt as he looked at her with shock and amazement at her statement. The more he stared into her eyes, he began to see her in a different light. He realized at that moment that Tisha didn't have any feelings for him at all. It became painfully clear to him right then and there, that she had been using him all along for his money. Tony had spent a total of $8,675 on a woman who claimed she wanted to spend the rest of her life with him, but wouldn't even kiss him.

He was very depressed now. To think that he had wasted time, money, and his emotions on someone who might already have somebody else or didn't even find him desirable. Tony later found out that Tisha only seriously dated men who lived out of town. Tisha had at least seven different boyfriends that all lived in different states and sent for her on occasion. She told all of them the same story, that she loved them and would very much like to spend the rest of her life with them.

Tisha would never let her men come to visit her. She'd tell them that she hated her hometown and coming to visit them was just the type of getaway she needed. She gave all of them the hard luck stories when she wanted money to go shopping. She had one boyfriend to pay the rent, another to pay her car note and the others to pay the rest of her bills. Tisha's game was unique in that her out of town men stood a very slim chance of ever crossing paths. She'd never wanted an everyday man. She liked having her space during the week and getting her groove on whenever she was sent for. She also liked the idea of being taken care of from afar off. Meanwhile, Tony tried to regain his self-esteem and restore his trust in women.

Hurricane Reyna: Dark Clouds Forming

Kevin and Reyna were in the car about to leave their job when Reyna looked over at Tommy, who was pulling up in the car next to them. Tommy worked at Kevin's company. Reyna blurted out, "Men are such dogs." Kevin replied, "Baby, why did you say that?" Reyna responded, "That guy over there named Tommy just called me twenty minutes ago and asked me if he could take me out. Now he is over there talking to Rhonda." Tommy had been dating Rhonda. Kevin wondered that if Reyna was supposed to be his lady, why was she so concerned with what was going on in another man's vehicle. Kevin asked Reyna if she wanted him to tell Tommy not to call her any more. Reyna just sat there staring out of the window and didn't even respond to Kevin. Kevin then asked Reyna if she had ever dated Tommy and Reyna quickly said, "No." She did confess that he had come into her reception area once and said, "You need to get your nails done," and threw twenty-five dollars on her desk. One other time he picked up lunch and brought it back to her. Kevin said, "And what else has he done for you? " Reyna said "Oh yeah, and he called me a couple of times at work, but he was just being silly."

The following day, Kevin got off work and noticed Reyna leaning over all inside Tommy's car talking to him. Kevin was on his way to pick up Reyna's son but Reyna was not off the clock yet. Kevin signaled for Reyna to come to him and asked her why was she over there talking to Tommy. Reyna replied, "He called me over to his car." Kevin said, "If he wants to talk to you, he should get out of his car and come to you. That just doesn't look real lady-like with you leaning all inside of his car that way." Reyna told Kevin that he was trippin'. Kevin asked Reyna if Tommy was trying to get with her. Reyna replied, "Yeah, can you blame him?" Kevin then asked, "Then why are you entertaining his game? You have a man." Reyna told Kevin that it was up to her to put Tommy in his place and for him not to worry about it. Kevin said, "Well, out of respect for our relationship, I don't want you talking to him anymore." Reyna said, "Okay, fine Kevin. I won't do anything more than speak to him."

Over the next couple of weeks, Tommy came up to the job at 4 p.m., the same time that Kevin got off work and Reyna took her break. It was starting to cause problems in the relationship. Kevin would talk to Reyna about it and she would tell him that he was just jealous. Reyna had begun to try and cover things up by standing under a tree while Tommy parked his car about five feet away from her. Kevin could still look out of the window and see them holding a conversation. As he was pulling out of the parking lot he looked to his left and there was Reyna leaning in Tommy's car. Kevin decided not to confront them; he was too angry. Instead he just drove home. Reyna called Kevin later that evening. She assumed that something was wrong because he was very short with her on the telephone.

Reyna pleaded with Kevin to tell her what was wrong and Kevin finally told her that he had seen her leaning into Tommy's car earlier that afternoon. Reyna then replied, "How? What were you doing, spying on me?" Kevin described how he had seen her, and Reyna said that she was sorry. About a week later, Kevin was leaving the job when he heard Tommy calling Reyna to his car. Kevin saw Reyna headed in that direction and asked Reyna to come to him. She ignored him and continued to walk to Tommy's car. Kevin said, "Reyna don't walk up to that nigga's car!" Reyna kept walking towards Tommy's car, while Tommy and his boys laughed at Kevin. Kevin heard Tommy say, "That nigga be hating, dog." Kevin and Tommy exchanged words and Reyna walked off. Kevin tried to catch up to Reyna but she slammed the office door in his face. Two months passed after that incident. They put some space between them for awhile. Kevin and Reyna both left the company. Now that they no longer have the stress of working together, they're beginning to enjoy each other again. Reyna has a new telephone number and things seem to be good.

Kevin, Reyna and Jason spent a Friday evening hanging out with Reyna's mom. Kevin dropped Reyna and her son off at home. Reyna told Kevin that she needed some money to take her son to the zoo or somewhere while Kevin was working. He reached into his pocket and gave her a one-hundred-dollar bill. Reyna asked Kevin to guess who called her and asked her to borrow some money. Kevin said, "Who baby?" Reyna replied, "Tommy." She said that she told him, "You know that I don't have any money, but if I did you would be good for it." Kevin just couldn't believe that she told him that. That means that Tommy had her home telephone number, and not only that, it is her new telephone number. Kevin dropped Reyna off and didn't say a word. However, on his way home, he realized that Reyna had been dishonest with him. Kevin called Reyna and asked her how Tommy got her telephone number. She said that she needed a ride from work, one day, and he had to ask her about something. "I forgot what." Kevin asked Reyna why she needed a ride, when he had already bought her a car.

Kevin snapped that Reyna knew that he and Tommy almost got into a physical confrontation and she was mingling with the enemy. "And what was he doing asking you for money, when I basically take care of Jason? Is he the pimp? What am I, the trick? This is a slap in my face." Reyna shouted some obscenities and hung up the telephone in Kevin's face. He called Reyna back and said, "I'm on my way to get my money back." Reyna said, "You can forget that one hundred dollars that you gave me, and if you come over acting like a fool, I'm calling the police." Kevin just turned on his TV and stayed up the entire night. He called Reyna early the next morning and begged to see her. She gave in after about the fourth call and told him to come on over. Kevin brought Reyna and Jason breakfast and told Reyna that he was sorry and he didn't care about that situation anymore, even though, he was very distraught about the entire situation.

"Silent Night, Lonely Night"

It was the worst holiday of Kevin's life. It was a cold Christmas Eve, when Jason's father came into town. Reyna told Kevin that she would appreciate it if he allowed her to call him while he was in town and if he could stop by. Kevin replied, "That's fine, as long as you promise me he won't spend the night." Reyna said that she didn't know where he would stay while he was in town, but he would not stay with her. She said "He is from this town and he has friends and family here, so that won't happen." Reyna told Kevin once before that if Jason's father found out about another man around his child, that he wouldn't give her any money towards Jason's support. Kevin felt that as long as he was taking care of her and Jason and being a role model in his life, she didn't need to beg his father to take care of him. If it became a big enough issue, he advised her to file on him so he wouldn't have a choice. Reyna however, felt like that if she filed on him, he would quit his job. Kevin decided not to rock the boat.

During the holidays, he bought Reyna five gifts for Christmas. He started giving her one present per day starting December 20. He wanted Christmas to be a week-long experience. Kevin gave Reyna a Coach purse, diamond earrings, a diamond ring, a gift certificate and her favorite perfume. He didn't hear from Reyna at all on Christmas Eve. He spent the night tossing and turning and shedding some tears. He sat at home waiting by the telephone, but Reyna never called. She finally called him about 3 p.m. on Christmas day. He was irritated and Reyna admitted to Kevin that her son's father had spent the night. On Christmas day, the day before Kevin's birthday, again he didn't see Reyna. He got his first chance to see Reyna on his birthday at work. Once again, he didn't have the opportunity to wake up with her on his birthday because her son's father was there. This experience destroyed Kevin. After this fiasco, Kevin lost weight and everyone was telling him that he looked stressed out.

Kevin took Reyna's word that her son's father slept in the living room and he and Jason just stayed up watching movies. However, deep down, Kevin didn't believe her. The only thing that kept Kevin and Reyna together was the love that Kevin had for

Reyna.

Kevin remembered promising Reyna that if she came up with four hundred dollars, he would give her the rest for a down payment on a new car. It was exactly a week after Christmas that Reyna called Kevin and said, "Guess what, I have my money." Kevin replied, "Have your money to do what?" Reyna said, "I have my four hundred dollars to help get me a car." This was a bad time for Kevin since he had just spent thousands on Reyna and her son for Christmas. However, he thought, don't ever make a promise you can't keep. He didn't know how he was going to come up with the money, but he did. Kevin took his entire paycheck, along with some money that he already had. He also pawned some things that were very dear to him. Kevin felt that he should do this because he had just given her an engagement ring last week, consequently, he just got further into debt. He never knew how hard it could be to take care of a woman and do everything that he could to spoil her.

Kevin made over forty thousand dollars that year, by working two jobs, hustling, and selling his valuables. He did not have a penny left in the bank. So off to the dealership they went. Reyna was determined to get a car that day. Kevin said, "Why don't we look around?" Reyna got pissed. Kevin compared their relationship to Burger King, she always had it her way. At times it seemed liked she tuned into one station, WIIFM (What's In It For Me?). Kevin went ahead and bought Reyna a car. It was a year old. On the bright side, Reyna wouldn't have to use Kevin's car anymore.

It was Monday morning when Reyna called Kevin and asked him what time he would be coming to work. He told her that he didn't know but that he might come in early to review some collection files. Something told Kevin to go to work early and he did. Upon arriving to work, Kevin saw Reyna getting out of a blue Honda Accord with tinted windows. He couldn't tell who was driving the car. He followed the car a couple of lights and saw that it was a brother with a hat on. He could not believe that two days after he had helped her purchase a car and one-week after he had given her an engagement ring, she was going to lunch with somebody else. That explained why she asked what time he was coming to work. Reyna's excuse was that they were just friends, she said he had a daughter and stopped by to give her son an invitation to his daughter's party. Kevin wasn't having it. He had already promised to take her to get insurance on her car when they got off from work. He stopped by her house to drop off her car. He told Reyna that it was over. "You turn me on when you're mad," replied Reyna as her eyes locked his in a steady gaze. Reyna began to take off all of her clothes and took his pants off. She began to give him a blowjob. Then she got on top and rode Kevin for ten minutes. Suddenly she got up and Kevin asked, "Where are you going?" Reyna said, "I thought it was over." Kevin said, "I forgive you." I don't know what she did, but he had to make love to her that moment, and now they are back together.

Tony: From the frying pan to Beatrice

Six months have passed since Tony and Tisha broke up. Tony hasn't been on a date since. Tony stayed to himself, and has yet, to come across a woman he is interested in. He decided to go to a get-together with some friends one Saturday. He really tried to get his friends to leave the party early because he wanted to go home until 11:30 pm when he laid eyes on Beatrice. She had a smile that could light up a dark alley. She had baby smooth skin with pretty brown eyes. Beatrice had hair that was so pretty that it invited you to run your fingers through it. Tony was fortunate that night because one of the girls with Beatrice knew Tony. He asked Felicia to introduce him and Felicia granted Tony that request. Tony and Beatrice laughed and joked all night long. He was surprised that she was so laid back and down to earth. Shortly thereafter, Tony's boys asked him if he was ready to go and Tony said, "Hell no!"

Tony was overjoyed. He thought Tisha was the most beautiful woman in the world, until he met Beatrice. Tony said that appearance was no longer the #1 priority with him. Beatrice, however, was not only beautiful but, had the most radiant personality he had ever seen. Tony hadn't laughed that much with anyone since he was a kid. He said that he felt like he could completely be himself with Beatrice.

One-week later, Tony planned to spend a quiet evening at home alone. He got a phone call from

Beatrice asking him if he wanted to go to a fraternity party. Tony hated frats, but would go to hell if Beatrice would join him, so of course, Tony agreed. He made a joke and said, "I hope I'm not taking you there to meet your man." Beatrice started laughing. Beatrice then responded, "I don't have a man, not yet anyway." Tony felt like a fat man at a buffet when Beatrice made such an insensitive comment.

They decided to do the double date thing. Beatrice brought Felicia and Tony brought Keith. First, they went to dinner and had drinks. Tony was so happy, he paid for everybody, and then it was off to the party. Tony had told Keith earlier, "Let's not sweat them at the party and give them some space; young ladies like that." Tony did dance with Beatrice a couple of times, but didn't get bothered by her dancing with other guys. Beatrice and Felicia told Tony and Keith that they would meet them at the car. Upon walking to the car, Tony saw Beatrice talking to a guy in the car next to his, but he wasn't bothered. Beatrice told Tony she needed her purse out of the trunk. Tony gave Beatrice her purse and Beatrice said she was leaving with Wayne. At this point he was puzzled. He asked Beatrice who Wayne was and she replied that he was an old friend. Felicia stepped in and told Beatrice to get in the car but she refused. Tony pleaded with Beatrice to get in the car. Meanwhile, the fraternity that was having the party had started to gather around Tony's car. Once again, Felicia shouted, "Beatrice, they have been good to us, get in the damn car!" Then one of the fraternity guys shouted, "She chose my boy, so y'all get the fuck out of here, before we crank this bitch up." Tony drove off and did not call Beatrice again, nor did Beatrice call him. Beatrice did, however, apologize to Tony through Felicia.

MY PIE

I feel as though I had a piece of pie,

just a fork full.   Enough to make me hungry,

but not enough to make me full.

This pie is so special, I could never get enough.

This pie is beautiful, with it's light dreamy crust.

I couldn't share this pie, because of its inner filling.

Filling made so sweet, filling made just for me.

I hope you understand how much I love my pie.

That's why I'll enjoy it till the day I die.

CHAPTER II

Love is Not Forever

Kevin and his brother Eric are starting to bond as of late. Eric is five years older than Kevin. Eric has three kids and has been married for eight years. He worked part-time hoping to get on full-time with his company. Eric had wanted to work full-time for his company since he got out of high school, but you usually have to work your way up to get on full-time. In the beginning, Eric was only working three hours a day and was struggling financially. He and his wife Sarah had just bought a house and with the three children and both their car payments, they were really feeling the pressure. Sarah had to hold down the fort while Eric worked diligently to get on full-time. She had a decent full-time job, but had a hard time managing her money.

Eric began to spend more time with Kevin. Eric and Kevin weren't very close growing up, because Eric was older and always had a girlfriend to occupy his time. Kevin was very shy around his family, but was a very fun person to hang out with among his friends. As time passed, Kevin and Eric became so close, they begin to go out together and confide in each other. Kevin nor Eric knew that the other was so much fun to hang out with. Kevin always thought Eric was just popular because of sports and because he was considered handsome. According to Kevin, Eric would do a lot of sleeping around the house, and Eric thought Kevin was just a shy bookworm. Kevin ended up giving Eric a key to his apartment. One day out of the blue, Eric called Kevin and told him that a lot of strange numbers had been appearing in Sarah's pager and her cellular phone. Kevin advised Eric not to check her pager or the phone numbers that were appearing on the phone bill. Kevin consoled Eric. "Hey, Sarah loves you and besides, that's an invasion of her privacy."

A week later, Eric decided to check Sarah's voice mail and heard some guy leaving her a message about the wonderful time he had and that he hoped to see her again soon. All of this was going on while Kevin was at school. When he returned home, he saw a lot of boxes, a weight set, and all of Eric's clothes in his apartment. Kevin said to himself, "Damn, I said you could have a key, but I didn't say you could move in." Kevin called his mother, who told him that Sarah had been having an affair and told Eric that she wanted a divorce. Eric showed up later at the apartment looking downcast. The one major difference between Eric and Kevin is that Kevin is so emotional that he cries when he is hurt, and Eric hasn't cried since he was a baby.

That night was the first time Kevin ever saw Eric cry. Kevin took Eric to a nearby topless club, and tried to shower his brother with drinks and table dances, but the pain was written all over his face. For the next couple of weeks, Kevin cooked meals fit for a king for Eric on a daily basis. Kevin felt that a home cooked meal was a good remedy for any problem. Sarah often called Kevin's house to tell Eric what a poor excuse for a man he was for working part-time. She was constantly telling him that he needed to be a man for once in his life. Eric would just hold the phone, while tears ran down his face. Kevin would always tell Eric to just hang up the phone and not listen to the negative criticism. Eric just held the phone, and took the abuse. Sarah would tell Eric how she left him because she needed a real man, not a boy. His scars will probably never heal. One thing Kevin could say about Eric was that he loved Sarah and his children, and Eric was far from lazy. He struggled through high school but persevered until he finished. Eric has been with his company for six years part-time, and had finally gotten hired on full-time with a salary increase to $45,000 a year. As they say, you never know what somebody will become if you give up on them too quickly. Eric is back on track, has his own place now, and is doing very well financially. The guy Sarah left Eric for has dumped her.

Meanwhile, Tony is starting to feel like everybody has someone but him. Tony's little brother Steve is a freshman in high school and he has his first girlfriend. Steve believes that women don't mess up relationships, the men they date mess up the relationship. Steve and Tony aren't that close, so they don't discuss their problems with each other. Steve is very close to his aunts, of which he has seven. He has witnessed how bad the men in their lives have treated them and has made a commitment to himself that he would be just the opposite of the men his aunts have dated. Steve's newly found love is Rebecca, a freshman at his school. They have been dating for about three months. Steve met Rebecca in his Physical Science class. He was the class clown, always making jokes to add spice to his teacher's lectures, but was an above average student. Rebecca, although she sat on the other side of the classroom, thought Steve was hilarious. She started waiting for Steve after class and they began to get to know each other. Steve thought the world of Rebecca not only because she was beautiful, but also because of her sense of humor. After two weeks of dating, Steve and Rebecca became an item. Steve was so ecstatic to have his first relationship that he told everybody in his family about her.

One cold day in December, Steve came down with the flu. He had to miss a couple of days of school, but Rebecca called him every night to check on him. Steve gave his dad some money and asked him to buy Rebecca a teddy bear and some candy so Steve could give them to her at school the next day. Steve saved his lunch money for three weeks to be able to buy Rebecca those gifts. He went to school rejuvenated to see Rebecca and to give her a surprise. Steve went to his locker to grab some books and found that all of Rebecca's things had been removed from the locker. He saw Rebecca, but she was holding hands with his teammate. There Steve was, holding a big teddy bear and a big box of heart-shaped candy. He couldn't do anything but walk off with his head down. He saw another girl that looked unhappy, so he decided to give her the candy and the teddy bear. He ran to the bathroom, sat in a stall, and cried for the next two class periods. When Steve saw Rebecca later and asked her why she left him, she replied that she didn't owe him an explanation. When Steve got home from school his dad asked, "What's wrong with you? You look like you lost your best friend." Steve never told his father. He did tell his mom however, and asked her not to tell his dad, but she told him anyway. For the next several months his dad made jokes about Steve getting dumped. Those jokes were very painful to Steve. Later he found out that Rebecca and his teammate broke up after two weeks. At a young age, Steve now sees women in a different light. He no longer saw women as innocent victims of men and their doggish ways. He now believes that men can also be victims.

Too good to last . . . . .

Steve's friend, Shawn, recalls the first time he fell in love. It was homecoming weekend at Shawn's college. Shawn had been without a companion for three years. He is a very picky individual, so it is very difficult for him to find someone he liked. Shawn was off at college and away from home for the first time. He had just witnessed his football team win its first homecoming game in four years, so the school was really pumped.

The parking lot was packed with people drinking and smoking by their cars. Shawn talked with Bruce, one of his best friends from back home, drank a beer, and talked to a couple of ladies. Shawn couldn't tell how the ladies looked because their backs were turned. Shawn approached Bruce and gave him a hug and then he noticed one of the ladies to be exceptionally gorgeous. Shawn whispered to Bruce to get the story on the honey who caught his eye. Bruce recalled that she attended school back home and that she was just one of his home-girls. Shawn began to socialize with the lady, who said her name was Crystal. Shawn asked Crystal if she was in a relationship and if she would be interested in getting to know him. She told Shawn that she was single and perhaps they could get to know one another better. Shawn couldn't locate a pen to get Crystal's telephone number, but Crystal told Shawn that he could get her number from Bruce. In Shawn's mind, he really didn't think a woman of Crystal's beauty and intelligence could be interested in him.

About a week after they met, Shawn called Bruce, to shoot the breeze, having forgotten about trying to get Crystal's telephone number. Bruce, however, told Shawn that Crystal had been bugging him everyday about whether Shawn had called him yet to get her phone number. Shawn was exultantly proud and joyful; so he got Crystal's telephone number and told Bruce he would talk to him later. Shawn called

Crystal long distance and she sounded ecstatic to hear from him. He was so elated that she was happy to hear from him. They exchanged addresses and phone numbers and from that point on for about a month, Shawn and Crystal talked or wrote each other daily. Shawn decided to go home for the weekend to see Crystal and they really hit it off. He took her by his parent's house and they just loved her. Later, when Shawn met Crystal's parents, they also adored him. Shawn and Crystal became best friends in a short period of time. Shawn began to come home every weekend to visit Crystal. They spent the entire weekend together.

Shawn and Crystal went to church together on Sundays, because they both believed that a couple that prayed together stayed together. Crystal sung in her church choir, and seemed to be a dedicated Christian. Shawn participated in a bible study at his college and was very much in touch with the Lord. Shawn and Crystal decided against having pre-marital sex, although they both had engaged in sexual activities in the past. He told Crystal everything about himself and she shared her inner most thoughts with him. If any relationship was perfect, they would have been up for the award. They celebrated their one-year anniversary with Shawn giving Crystal a gold ring. He told Crystal that he may not have a lot, but one day, he would give her the world. Shawn always spent his last to take Crystal out, or surprised her with a gift.

Three had months passed since Shawn gave Crystal the ring. She had began acting peculiar. She told Shawn that he shouldn't come home every weekend and that she needed some space. She stopped calling Shawn and writing to him as well. When he wanted to talk to her he had to initiate the call. Every time Shawn spoke to her she had very little to say. He pleaded with her on several occasions to tell him what was wrong, but she would always say nothing was wrong. Shawn told Crystal if there was anything he could do, he would. He also told her that they could get counseling at the church, but Crystal declined to go to counseling. Shawn decided to call Bruce to see if he knew anything. Bruce told Shawn that Crystal met a guy named Wayne who was about to get drafted into the NFL. Bruce also told him that Crystal liked the guy, but didn't know how to tell him or how to break up with him. Crystal said that Shawn didn't do anything wrong, so she didn't know what to do. Shawn thanked Bruce and told him he would call him later. Shawn immediately got on his knees and asked God for some guidance. He continued to call Crystal to try to work things out, but she showed no interest in continuing their relationship. He got so frustrated knowing Crystal no longer wanted him that he asked her if she wanted out of their relationship and she told him that she did. Shawn knew he gave the relationship all he had, but that he couldn't compete with a pro athlete. Shawn called Bruce and told him that they were no longer together and Bruce told Shawn that he knew. Bruce also told him that the pro scouts had called Crystal, to ask her questions about

Wayne. Shawn agreed that Crystal must be pretty impressed.

A month passed and Shawn witnessed Wayne become a six-round draft pick of the Washington Redskins. Shawn decided to go to the mall one Saturday afternoon and saw Crystal walking in the mall dressed in Wayne's Washington Redskins jersey and they had a brief conversation. Crystal asked Shawn how had he been doing and Shawn asked Crystal how she and Wayne were doing, with his voice crackling. Crystal talked about Wayne with so much excitement and energy, Shawn had to cut the conversation short. Shawn couldn't believe that they used to pray together and talked about a future with each other. He decided not to date anymore, because he literally lost his best friend.

A year went by and Shawn still had not gone on a single date. He noticed in the sports page that Wayne was waived after playing one year in the NFL. Shawn later learned from Bruce that Crystal and Wayne were no longer together. Shawn knew in his heart that he still loved Crystal, but his pride would not allow him to go back to her.

Of Course I Love You,
Under These Conditions . . . .

Shawn decided after a year and three months without a date, that it was time for him to go out again. He was introduced to a model named Angela through a friend. He took Angela to a five-star restaurant over-looking the lake. He told Angela that he had just graduated from college and was hoping to get accepted into a physical therapy school. Angela was an aspiring model, hoping for that one big break. Shawn told her that he didn't have a lot of money, but he could afford to take a young lady out and show her a nice time. Angela seemed to be turned on by Shawn's down to earth attitude. Angela told Shawn that he was very refreshing and that she would love to spend more time with him. He explained that he had a good work ethic and a lot of potential, but he couldn't find a woman to stand by his side until he made it. Angela said, "That's not a problem, you've just been dating the wrong women."

For the next six months Shawn and Angela were inseparable. Shawn couldn't believe he was back in a relationship. He felt there was another person in his life to call baby, pooh, honey, sweetheart, etc., and another person to call him by a pet name. When would the vicious cycle end? Who was going to be his last baby? Shawn fell in love quickly. Angela told Shawn everyday how much she loved him. Shawn's life was looking up! He finally got accepted into a one-year physical therapy continuing education program. Shawn had been waiting on this since he first enrolled in college. He had dreams of owning a sports medicine facility. The only problem about the physical therapy program was that it was full time from 8 a.m. to 5 p.m., and required a minimum of three hours of homework every night. This meant Shawn had to give up his good job with the state. He had saved his money wisely and therefore had enough to pay his rent and other bills for a year.

He now had to manage on a fixed budget. He knew that he wouldn't be able to wine and dine Angela while he was in school, it just wasn't economically feasible. Shawn couldn't wait to tell Angela the good news about being accepted into the program.

Shawn invited Angela over for a candle light dinner later that evening. As soon as Angela walked through the door, Shawn busted out his news about his acceptance. Angela gave Shawn a big hug and a kiss. He explained the amount of hours involved in the program and Angela responded, "What are you going to do for work?" Shawn explained that if he stayed within his budget, he would have enough money to live on for a year. By now Angela had a sour look on her face. Shawn noticed her change of expression and responded, "I love you, I know I won't be able to wine and dine you like I have been, but when I graduate, I will spoil you beyond imagination." He told Angela that he would like to spend the rest of his life with her, and that this was something he had to do for both of them to live comfortably. He told her that he understood if she could not deal with him not working and he'd also understand if she didn't want to give up her lifestyle for one year. Angela responded that she cared about him deeply and wished him the best, but she just couldn't date an unemployed brother. She asked, "What if you start trying to use my salary to finance your education?" Shawn said that wouldn't happen. Angela told Shawn that they would always be friends, but she didn't want to go through a relationship like that. Angela began to gather her belongings that she had in Shawn's home. Shawn thought to himself that he knew a Black woman would-n't stand by his side in his time of need, and although he'd told Angela that he would understand, he really didn't. Angela left, without even eating the dinner Shawn had cooked for her. He sat in his apartment and cried while he drank the entire bottle of wine by himself.

Two weeks went by and Shawn started school. He had difficulty concentrating in class and studying at home, because all he could think about was Angela. Shawn was very capable of passing, but his concen-tration level was gone. He eventually flunked out of the program, and he had no job, no companion, no money, and didn't accomplish what he set out to do.

Roxanne, Roxanne, Can I Be Your Second Man?

Meanwhile, Tony claimed that he was very con-tent being single at this stage in his life. He admitted that he fantasized almost daily about being with one of his co-workers, Roxanne, but she was married. Tony said that Roxanne reminded him of Janet Jackson, with a very out-going personality. Tony had never been with a married woman, and didn't feel that it would be morally right if he pursued her. He believed in the old adage that you reap what you sow. So Tony decided that Roxanne wasn't an option for him outside of his imaginative mind.

One rainy Tuesday evening Tony's friend Mike came to him and said that Roxanne's husband ran off and left her and her son. Roxanne's husband had gone back to his home state. Mike Tony that Roxanne was so upset that she had been crying non-stop. Tony felt that the situation was screwed up, but being very sensitive to other people's problems, didn't see it as an opportunity to take advantage of Roxanne. Tony however, asked Roxanne if she wanted to go to breakfast when they got off. He told her that he would be there if she needed a shoulder to cry on. Roxanne accepted Tony's offer, stating that she needed some coffee and somebody there to listen to her. Tony has somewhat of a comical personality, so even though Roxanne was devastated about her situation, she couldn't help but laugh with him. They both seemed to have genuinely enjoyed each other's company that day. Tony was the type that didn't stand out in crowds, because he is so laid back, but he was very entertaining in one-on-one conversations. The night ended with Tony giving Roxanne his telephone number as he told her to call if she needed anything. Surprisingly, Roxanne felt a lot lighter and she was able to go straight home to get some rest.

Tony contemplated whether or not he could accept just being her friend, knowing that he was very attracted to her. He realized that if he messed around with a married woman, that God wouldn't bless him. In spite of all of the bad relationships he had gone through, he felt a spiritual conviction when he went against the will of God. Somehow, he could hear one of his Pastor's sermons or recall a scripture in the bible that tugged at him and wouldn't let him have any peace. Tony tried to rationalize with himself that what he was doing was not really that bad. He ran into Roxanne the very next day in the building where they both worked. Tony and Roxanne began to talk and he couldn't help but notice how exceptionally beautiful Roxanne looked. He wanted to ask her out for the weekend, but didn't want to offend her. Inn addition, he was feeling really shy. He finally mustered up enough courage to ask Roxanne hypothetically if a platonic friend asked her out for dinner and a movie if she would go. Roxanne responded that it depended on who that friend was. She caught on to Tony after about ten minutes, and asked, "Tony do you want to take me to the movies?" Tony replied, "And if I do?" Roxanne answered, "I would go with you." Tony asked, "Will you go out with me on Saturday?" Roxanne agreed. Tony had his first official date with a woman that he had admired for more than a year.

That Saturday night, Tony looked out of his window in anticipation of Roxanne coming over for their date. Roxanne was supposed to meet Tony at his house at 6:30 that evening, but she didn't arrive until 6:45. To Tony, who anxiously anticipated her visit, it felt like hours. Roxanne knocked lightly on the door, and there she was with a nice fitting wrap-around skirt, open-toe sandals, and the most beautiful feet Tony had ever seen. He could tell her feet had received a professional pedicure because they looked like feet that had never walked on a hard surface. Roxanne's legs looked like she had carefully rubbed them with baby oil and she smelled so good, Tony just wanted to tenderly embrace and kiss her. Instead he walked her to his car and accidentally bumped into her while opening the door for her. He was so turned on by Roxanne that he immediately had an erection. She felt so soft that he thought he would burst. Tony and Roxanne enjoyed the movies and dinner and decided they would go to the park to watch the stars. He sat on the bench with Roxanne thinking how nice it would be just to hold her hand. Tony asked Roxanne if she had a nice time and Roxanne blushed, "You were great company tonight." Tony said, "Yeah right." Roxanne said, "I'm serious," and reached over and gave him the most luscious kiss he had ever experienced. That day he learned what it was like to see the stars. They were both aroused and talked about how they both wanted to get to know each other more intimately. Roxanne told Tony that she would love to have sex with him, but she was on her period. She told Tony that even though she was married, she had always admired him and thought he was very handsome. Tony was absolutely shocked, and revealed to Roxanne that he had several fantasies about her and thought she was the most beautiful woman that he had seen in quite some time.

Roxanne confided in Tony that her mother had gone through a situation similar to the one that she was now faced with. Roxanne compared dating Tony to her deceased mother's situation. "My stepfather was a wonderful man. I'm just wondering if my getting to know you is a blessing from God, because your mannerisms are very similar to my stepfather's." Tony took it as a great compliment and was also happy about her mentioning that maybe it was a sign from

God. It made Tony feel a little better about being with a married woman. Roxanne told Tony that she would make love to him in a couple of days and that she would spend the night with him if he agreed. Tony quickly stated that he would love for her to spend the night with him.

When Tony got back to work, his friend Mike told him that Roxanne had siad what a great time she had with him over the weekend, and Mike told Tony that Roxanne really thought he was very special. Tony was so happy that Roxanne liked him, that he went against his fundamental beliefs to date her. Roxanne decided to spend the night with Tony on Wednesday. She came over to Tony's place with an overnight bag and told him that she needed to take a shower. Roxanne stepped out of the bathroom dressed in a satin red nightgown and immediately began to seduce Tony. She started at Tony's neck and worked her way to his chest and began to play with his navel before getting to the element of surprise. Roxanne began to use her tongue and lips to work magic and bring him pleasure. Tony almost totally blacked out. He had experienced eroticism below the navel several times in his life, but none compared to this. Just when Tony thought it couldn't get any better, Roxanne slowly guided him inside her and Roxanne, who is five years older than Tony, gave him the ride of his life. He was totally whipped at that point. One thing he knew for sure, he was addicted to Roxanne. For the next four months Tony and Roxanne were totally inseparable.

Daddy, Daddy, Daddy!

Roxanne decided it was time to invite Tony over to her house for dinner. He went over after church on Sunday, and Roxanne's son, Brad, opened the door. Tony shook Brad's hand and sat on the couch, when out came Reese in a diaper. Tony said, "This must be Reese," and Roxanne said, "Yes, this is my baby." Tony then asked, "Who was that, who opened the door?" and Roxanne said that it was her son, Brad. Tony said, "I thought you only had Reese," and she said, "No, I have three children." Tony said, "Who is the other child?" Roxanne said, "Brandy. I never told you about Brandy?" and Tony said, "No, only about Reese." At this point, Tony wondered what he'd gotten himself into." He never thought that he would date someone with three children. He knew there was no turning back since he had already committed himself. He had stayed up many nights listening to Roxanne cry about her husband and had consoled her.

Tony knew how many times he had been hurt, and he felt that as long as she was on his team, that he would make sure neither of them would have to go through that kind of pain again. Besides, Tony was in love with Roxanne, and felt that her problems were his problems, and her past mistakes were just the past. Roxanne's children immediately took to Tony and Tony to them. Tony even began to coach Brad's baseball team because they were without one. Tony developed a real close relationship with Reese, who used to follow Tony around. Tony didn't have a real close relationship with Roxanne's daughter Brandy, but they got along. Roxanne had been upset with Brandy because she was flunking the fifth grade and it didn't seem likely that Brandy was going to advance to the sixth grade. Tony decided to help Brandy study everyday after school, and he also offered her money as an incentive for getting good grades. Tony worked with Brandy, to the point where she became an "A" & "B" student for the first time in her life. Tony and Roxanne became so close that they exchanged keys to each other's place of residence. Tony eventually told Roxanne that he would pay for her divorce, and that he wanted to marry her. He realized that this was a big sacrifice because he didn't have any children of his own and he didn't want to have more than three children when he got married. Tony told Roxanne that they didn't have to have any children together, and that he would treat her kids as if they were his own. He felt in his heart that Roxanne was a good woman, and no matter what the negatives were, he had never been with a woman that he could describe as a good woman. Roxanne had a big family, and some weekends she would drive down to see them and they would drive back down with her. Tony would stay at Roxanne's house and prepare large meals for twenty plus people. Roxanne's family adored Tony because he took good care of her and her kids. He didn't have many bills, so any extra money he had he gave to Roxanne.

That's Why They Call It the Blues

Roxanne had been home sick lately, so she asked Tony to buy her a plane ticket so she could go to visit her relatives. Tony told Roxanne, "Whatever you want baby, I'm here for you." Tony was aware that Roxanne's husband resided in her home state, but Roxanne said she hadn't had any contact with him. Tony bought Roxanne's ticket. She asked him if he would drop her off and pick her up from the airport and Tony insisted he wouldn't have it any other way. He bought a personal greeting card for her and made her a tape telling her how much he loved her and how much she would be missed with their favorite love songs playing at a low volume in the background. Tony placed the tape, along with five hundred dollars inside the card. They were very affectionate in the airport. He saw his minister at the airport and introduced Roxanne to him as his future wife. Tony handed Roxanne the card and told her he loved her with all his heart and that he had a good friend who was a divorce attorney that would work on her divorce as soon as she got back. Roxanne left and Tony's life seemed as if it were on hold, but Tony stayed at Roxanne's house so he could take care of her children.

Tony got only one phone call from Roxanne telling him that she had made it, and to check on the kids. Roxanne's brother called later to check on the kids and to tell Tony that Roxanne would be staying two extra days. Roxanne's brother gave Tony the new time to pick her up. Tony didn't understand why Roxanne didn't call herself, but he assumed she was just having fun and enjoying her family.

When the time came to pick Roxanne up from the airport, Tony got so excited that he passed up the airport. When Roxanne came through the gate, Tony ran up to her and picked her up off of her feet. However, Roxanne didn't look the least bit excited about seeing him. It was so evident that Tony had to ask her for a kiss. He could only feel his lips pressed against a pair of luscious, but non-responsive lips. Tony asked Roxanne what was wrong. She answered, "I'm just tired." He asked her if she talked to her husband, and Roxanne said yes. Tony asked Roxanne about starting the divorce proceedings, and she said she was not going through with it because her husband wanted joint custody of the kids and she couldn't be without her kids for half of the year. Tony also found out that only the youngest child actually belonged to her husband. Roxanne remained very distant toward Tony. He noticed the distance but tried to have sex with Roxanne, to no avail.

When they finally did engage in sex, Roxanne just laid there like a bump on a log, so Tony decided not to participate either. He realized that she didn't want to have sex, and was only doing it to avoid his questions about their relationship. Tony was really sick but hoped Roxanne would snap out of it. One week later, he rented some movies and decided to bring dinner by Roxanne's house. Tony sat on the couch with his arm around Roxanne while the kids slept. He asked her to tell him the truth about her husband and how it affected their relationship. Roxanne told Tony that her husband planned to move back to town. Tony asked, "Where is he going to stay?" Roxanne said in a low tone, that he planned to stay with her and that they were getting back together. Tony asked Roxanne, "When were you going to tell me?" Roxanne responded, "I don't know." Tears started to fall out of Tony's eyes and he made a move to leave, actually hoping Roxanne would stop him and tell him it wasn't so, but she didn't. He called her when he got home and she told him, that they could still kick it, but they would have to be on the down-low now. Tony told Roxanne that she had destroyed his life and she told him that he was being weak, and weak men turned her off. Tony called Roxanne a bitch out of anger, and she responded, "Are you just finding that out?"

Tony was so disturbed about his situation, that he sought psychiatric help, and had to take medication. Roxanne refused to give Tony any of his things. He didn't ask for the gifts that he bought her, because he believed that she should keep those things. The things she had asked to borrow, such as household items, CD's, videotapes, and shirts, he expected to be returned. Tony was advised not to get in contact with Roxanne anymore. He resigned from his job because he developed an ulcer. Roxanne tried to make Tony's life a living hell. He had to change his phone number to avoid any further confrontations. He no longer has any contact with Roxanne and vice-versa.

What You Don't Know Can Hurt You!

Kevin decided it was time to get Tony out of the house. Kevin was invited to a house party and wanted Tony to go with him. Kevin's intentions were to help Tony meet somebody since it had been a long time since Tony had been on a date. Once they got to the party, Kevin introduced Tony to every eligible woman he knew there. However, Tony didn't hit it off with any of the women he met. The host asked Kevin to go to the store to get some ice, which was cool with Kevin because he was only at the party to help Tony out. When Kevin got back to the party he spotted Tony against the wall talking to a woman that he remembered having a one-night stand with several years ago. Kevin went over and saw the look in Tony's eyes suggesting this is the one. The young lady's name was Linda, and she reached out to shake Kevin's hand. Tony asked Kevin and Linda if they knew each other and they responded that they did. Kevin proceeded to the kitchen to put the ice up. Tony and Linda hung out until it was time to go, and they exchanged telephone numbers.

On the ride home Tony kept telling Kevin how nice Linda was, but also kept asking Kevin if he had ever been with her. Kevin decided to lie to Tony, because he hadn't seen him that happy in a long time. Besides, Kevin didn't view Linda as a whore. He recalled being extremely drunk the night he met Linda, and he was licking his wounds from a prior relationship when his self-esteem was at an all-time low. Kevin met Linda at the apartment of one of his home-girls. It was getting late, so he volunteered to walk Linda back to her apartment, since she lived in the same complex as the person Kevin's home-girl. Kevin remembered being tipsy and so was Linda, he assumed.   He asked Linda if he could use her restroom and Linda invited him inside.

Linda wasn't very attractive to Kevin at all. She just wasn't his type, however, Kevin was very horny and it had been a while. Kevin asked Linda to put on some music and she did, while he began to massage her neck and shoulders. Kevin had relaxed Linda so well that she laid back on his chest. He kissed her on the forehead, then on the cheek, then they made eye contact, and began to really kiss her. Kevin tried to go all the way but Linda kept refusing. They sat up for hours and discussed having sex with a person you just met, weighing the pros and cons. During the discussion, they would take breaks to kiss and engage in a little foreplay. They got so hot and stimulated that Kevin went to his car to get a condom at 5:00 a.m. Eventually that situation turned into a one-night stand since they never exchanged telephone numbers or saw each other anymore until they met at the party. Kevin didn't look at Linda in a negative way, because he would have to see himself in the same light. Kevin's philosophy was that the man is just as responsible as the woman is when they engage in sexual activity. The man isn't a stud and the woman isn't a whore. It's just something that two people decide to do. Besides, Kevin knew she had really tried to fight the urge, and that counts for something. He decided he would let Tony get to know Linda for himself, and anyway, that episode happened four years ago, and people can really grow up in a short period of time.

Tony's first date with Linda was a drive-in movie. He had popped his trunk at the movies, and to Linda's surprise, he had a huge stuffed animal to give to her. Tony said, "Since it's too early for us to cuddle, I think you deserve to cuddle with someone." Their date went well, according to Tony. Later that week, Kevin got a strange call from Linda. He was surprised because he hadn't given her his telephone number. Tony had given Kevin's phone number to Linda, because she wanted to ask Kevin something. Linda wanted to know if Kevin had told Tony about their one night stand. Kevin told Linda that their history was in the past and that he would rather see her get to know Tony, a very good man with a lot of love to give. Kevin wished her the best. Tony and Linda began to see each other on a weekly basis. He seemed to be happy again, but Linda didn't seem quite as happy. Linda was going out with Tony because she didn't have any other options, plus Tony made her feel like a queen. Tony and Linda decided against having sex, which was okay with Tony. He was so excited about Linda, that he invited her to his family reunion and introduced her as his wife to be, if God said the same. Tony began to shower Linda with affection and she admitted that she had some feelings for him.

When Linda's birthday came, Tony made sure Linda had a special day. He asked Linda two weeks in advance if she would spend the day with him and she said, "Sure." Tony decided to buy Linda a tennis bracelet with some cash he had saved out of his last two pay checks and he also called the telephone company to get a two-week extension on his bill. Buying the tennis bracelet was a big sacrifice for Tony, but he remembered Linda complimenting a young lady's bracelet one evening when they were out.

Tony took the bracelet to her job, with a dozen red roses. Linda gave him a big hug, a smile and asked him what he had planned for the evening. He told Linda that he wanted to cook for her. Linda said, "That sounds good. What do you plan to cook?" Tony asked, "What is your favorite?" Linda replied, "Italian." Tony admitted that he was not the best chef in the world, but for Linda he promised to make a pasta dinner fit for a queen. Tony went home and called Kevin because Kevin had a really good spaghetti sauce recipe. Tony asked Kevin for his recipe and Kevin asked, "Why?" Tony explained, and Kevin volunteered to cook at Tony's house and leave, but Tony said he wanted to cook for his own lady. Kevin told Tony what to get at the store and gave Tony the directions for making his sauce. Several hours later, Tony called Kevin and said he had laid rose petals all over the house, and he had his fireplace going. He had a good bottle of red wine and candles lit throughout the apartment. Tony and Kevin talked for two hours without Tony hearing from Linda, so he decided to give her a call. Linda wasn't at home, so Tony tried paging her, but Linda didn't call back. At 11 p.m., Tony called Kevin and told him he had been stood up. Kevin did his best to console Tony, before finally saying, "Hey, bring the wine and spaghetti over so we can get our grub on." Tony was cool with the idea because he didn't want to be in the house alone. Kevin advised Tony not to call Linda anymore because she wasn't worth it. Tony agreed, until the next day, when he developed an irresistible urge to call Linda. Tony left the house and tried to call everybody he knew rather than call her. He periodically went by his house to check his caller ID and answering machine to see if Linda had called.

The day drug on, she hadn't called, and Tony truly wanted to know what had happened. He strongly believed that every relationship for whatever the reason it failed, needed closure. He started coming up with reasons to call her, like something could have happened to her. Kevin called to check up on Tony, who had received more calls than usual that day, but Tony was still waiting on Linda to call. Kevin said, "I know you're disappointed that I'm not Ms. wonderful. Believe me brother, I know what you're going through. You're suffering right now as a victim of someone else's insensitivity and selfishness." Tony asked Kevin if he should call Linda and Kevin said, "You're going to call regardless of what I tell you." Kevin added, "Honestly, I think she owes you the next call." Tony asked Kevin, "What if something happened to her?" Kevin replied, "Nothing ever happens to people who do other people wrong." Kevin said, "I don't believe in what goes around comes around anymore.

It just seems like people that hurt people continue to hurt person after person, and they seem to always date people that genuinely care about them." All the while that Kevin was speaking, Tony was thinking about calling Linda. He hung up the telephone with Kevin and immediately called her. She answered the telephone as if nothing had happened. Linda's excuse was that her mother took her to dinner and that her battery was running low on her pager. She figured that's probably why she didn't know he had called. Tony told Linda what he had prepared, and Linda replied, "Sorry, but I very rarely get to spend time with my mom." Tony and Linda never spoke again.

DON'T TOUCH ME

Please, Don't touch me!

For your love isn't permanent.

I don't want that feeling,

if it's your love that you are giving.

I know it's good, I had you in my head,

but love is eternal and flings are dead.

No, I can't live day to day.

Because I won't understand,

if you walk out of my life with another man.

So forgive me, shake my hand,

don't be mad, let's be friends.

CHAPTER III

Starting The New Year Off With A Fizzle

Christmas had just passed when Kevin received a telephone call from Reyna. She announced that she and Jason wanted to go home to see her family and the cost would only be four hundred and sixty-eight dollars. Kevin really did not have it, but he would pawn something of his if necessary so that he could please Reyna. He was a little disappointed, since this meant that he would not get to spend New Year's with Reyna and Jason. What was even more disturbing was that Reyna would be gone for almost two weeks and Kevin had built his life around her. A couple of days before it was time for Kevin to drop Reyna off at the airport. He gave Reyna some spending money and told Jason and Reyna to be careful because he loved them very much. Kevin went home and tried to adjust to being alone, but he couldn't. He ended up going to bed early at around 8:00 p.m. on New Year's Eve and every night for the entire week. He was miserable, and missed Reyna and Jason so much that he didn't know what to do.

Friday, the day that Kevin had waited for, finally arrived. It was time to pick up Reyna and Jason from the airport, and there was a delay in the flight. When Reyna's flight finally came in, he gave her and Jason a big hug. To Kevin's surprise, Reyna told him that she was going out of town that night for the weekend with the girls. Kevin said, "No." Reyna stated that they had already planned it and that she was going. He explained that he had plans and he missed his family and that he was standing his ground. Reyna said, "What do you mean?" Kevin replied, "You're so inconsiderate, it's always what you want. You never check on your man to see if he is okay or if he needs any attention." Reyna said, "You can say what you want Kevin, I'm going."

He dropped Reyna off at home, stopped by the liquor store, went home, and got drunk. After several drinks, he called Reyna and pleaded for her not to leave him because he missed her so much. Reyna said that she could not help that Kevin then did something that he thought that he would never do, maybe because he was drunk. He told Reyna it was over, that he had no more room in his heart for her selfish behavior. Reyna said, "Fine" and hung up the telephone. Kevin couldn't believe he was going to be off from work the next day and didn't have anything planned to do. He had no idea what he was going to do. When he and Reyna were together, he would keep Jason out of day care on his off days and would run errands for Reyna.

The next week Reyna called and asked Kevin

if he could get her car serviced on his day off. Kevin really didn't want to, but although they weren't together, he still loved her and tried to take care of her manly duties, so that she wouldn't have to ask anyone else. He didn't mind doing it for her, because he knew he could not mentally deal with another man being around her yet. So off to Reyna's job he went. He decided to park his car at Reyna's house since it was within walking distance of the building where Reyna worked. Kevin got the car keys from her, went to the dealership and waited for them to completely service her car. After the car had been serviced, he decided to clean it up, it was filthy. Kevin had to rush to pick Reyna up, so he didn't have time to put gas in the car, and the tank was almost empty. He picked her up and she said that she was going out of town to a wedding and that she was in a rush. Kevin said, "Well, I'll follow you to the gas station." First, he had to go back to her house to get his car. Reyna said, "Well let me run upstairs and get my clothes." She came down the stairs with every hoochie-mama outfit in her closet. The first thing that came to Kevin's mind was that she was going to shack up with a man for the weekend. He had just told himself that he needed to chill, that it was not his business.

Kevin couldn't even describe how he was feeling; he was so crushed. After he pumped the gas, Reyna tried to hug him, but Kevin told her to get away from him. Kevin told Reyna,"I know you're going to see another man." Reyna told him that he was crazy. The ride back to the house was the worst he had ever experienced. He cried all the way home. This was the first time since Kevin was a child that he had cried and moaned at the same time. He thought to himself that he had gotten her car serviced so she could go out of town to see another man. Kevin thought, "Hell, when we were together; I had to go see her most of the time. She would even complain about coming to visit me right here in town." He wondered to himself, "What does this man have that I don't have, when she would complain about a ten minute drive to come see me and didn't mind driving six hours to see him?" Kevin thought at first that he might be crazy for accusing her, but for the next eight weeks, Reyna went out of town on Fridays. She would go to the beauty shop on Thursday, and leave Friday after work. He knew she went to the beauty shop on Thursday because he would pass by the shop on his way home from work and see her car parked outside.

During that eight-week period he lost twelve pounds, didn't have a date, didn't shave, picked over his food and barely slept. Maybe Kevin was just old-fashioned, but he wouldn't start dating someone else as soon as he got out of a relationship. He thought it was best to make sure that he was making the right decision and that he didn't still have feelings for that person. He began to challenge God about the whole situation. His prayers went like this: "God, I know you can't take the feeling I have for Reyna away, but God can you at least help me live again? I feel like a dead man walking right now. If I ever felt like I don't have any self-esteem, this is the time."

RETURN TO THE SCENE OF THE CRIME

Kevin thought that God had intervened on his behalf and answered his prayers, because Reyna stopped going out of town and started investing her time in Kevin. They dated on a steady basis for the next three months. He decided that his love for Reyna was too strong and that he should let bygones be bygones. Kevin started back being his same usual self, taking care of Jason and making sure that Reyna didn't need anything. The relationship in Kevin's eyes was going as smooth as silk. He had just helped Reyna celebrate her birthday. He surprised her at work by bringing her a card, cake, and balloons. After work, he picked her up and took her to the lake, where he had prepared a picnic. He picked out a nice spot under a tree, where he laid out a blanket. In the cooler he had one red rose, some white wine, wine glasses, red grapes, green grapes, cherries, strawberries and an assortment of finger sandwiches. Kevin thought that he had really impressed Reyna and he made a commitment to be even more romantic this time around. Once Kevin and Reyna finished the picnic, he took Reyna shopping. He let her buy whatever she wanted. She ended up getting two outfits, two pairs of shoes, and a purse. Kevin also gave Reyna two hundred dollars to pay her bills. She had a wonderful birthday, and to show her gratitude, she went back to Kevin's place and made wonderful love to him.

Kevin really started to feel content and at ease, being with the woman that he loved. Reyna told him that she wanted to move in with him, when he bought his house in two months. She has also told him that she was his and that no other man could come between them. Kevin was very confident with his present situation. He did, however have a slight feeling that things were going a little too good, because everything seemed so right.

On Wednesday, Kevin stopped by Reyna's house to give her one hundred dollars. She wanted money to get her hair done and to have some spending change. When Kevin asked Reyna for a commitment again, Reyna said, "That's' so childish and old-fashioned." Reyna told him that she was his, but she didn't like commitments. Kevin was comfortable with that as long as he felt she was committed this time. He picked Reyna up for lunch on the following Thursday and they were very affectionate. Kissing and hugging one another, and Reyna ended the lunch by telling Kevin that she loved him. Kevin was so geeked up about their relationship that he was again seeing stars. Reyna called Kevin later that night and asked him if he would give her and Jason some money to go to the movies on Saturday, and Kevin agreed. He said he would love to take them Saturday morning, but he had to take defensive driving that weekend. She called Kevin on Friday and asked him out to lunch, but he couldn't meet her because he was involved in a family matter. Kevin's cousin was in town from college, to visit her mother who had cancer. Reyna knew Kevin was going through a lot of emotional distress with his aunt having cancer, and she promised to be there for him. He decided to take his cousin to the movies to get her mind off her problems. He left the theater in good spirits, feeling that he had helped his cousin to get her mind off her mother's illness. He saw at a distance one of his friends, Larry, at the theater. Larry had always been somewhat envious of Kevin. He used to have the nicest car among the fellows until Kevin bought his car. Larry had a habit of always challenging Kevin to all types of contests. He used to inquire about Reyna when they had split up. Occasionally Reyna would ask Kevin certain things about Larry. She admitted to him that Larry had asked her out to play cards, dominoes and other games. Kevin, however, didn't feel threatened, because Reyna claimed she wasn't attracted to light-skinned brothers. Larry drove a brand new convertible sports car with really dark tinted windows. Kevin noticed a woman on the passenger side whose hair style resembled Reyna's, the style that Kevin had just paid for at beauty shop. Kevin realized that they did not see him, so he drove back around. Larry recognized Kevin and threw the peace sign in the air. Larry motioned to Kevin that he couldn't roll the window down, signaling that he had marijuana smoke in the car. Kevin then got a better view of Reyna checking out the time of the movie. He had to have his cousin to drive around in the car because he was blocking traffic. Kevin approached Reyna and asked her, "What the fuck are you doing here with Larry?" and Reyna responded, "Don't try to front me, I'm not your woman." Kevin was shocked because now he realized what Reyna would say to him with her back against the wall. He watched Reyna get in Larry's car and close the door. Kevin's' jaw was pretty much on the ground at this point. He couldn't believe his friend is out with the woman he loved. Kevin tapped on Reyna's window, Reyna opened the door and responds, "Don't be tapping all on this man's window." Then Larry gets out the car and said, "Yeah, don't tap on my window you're just going to have to handle this another time." Kevin asked Larry, "What's up with this," his arms in the air, and they began to approach each other when a cop came up and said, "You guys break it up." Kevin then walked away.

Kevin paid for everything Reyna had on, including getting her hair and nails done. What bothered him more was when he went out with Reyna, she would just throw on anything, but on this day, she was dressed to impress. Kevin once again cried all the way home. He didn't go to sleep at all; he kept trying to call Reyna. Finally, at 3:30 a.m., a man answered, but it wasn't Larry. It was Reyna's child's father, Tyron, who said Reyna was not there. Reyna had told Kevin earlier in the week that Tyron got into it with his brother and his brother kicked him out. She told Kevin that Tyron came by one morning to take a shower but he couldn't stay. That was okay with Kevin since she was honest about Tyron being there. Reyna said that Tyron couldn't stay with her until he got a place. Kevin and Tyron talked until 7:00 a.m. They both decided to be honest and come at each other like men. Kevin discovered that they both were intimate with Reyna and that she had been leading both of them on. Kevin told Tyron about the incident at the movies and he said that Larry must have been who she was spending the night with lately. Tyron told Kevin about the out of town men and that it was more than one guy. Kevin told him about his suspicions of who she might be messing around with and together they came up with enough men to fill an NBA roster. Kevin gave Tyron some advice and vice-versa. They both concluded that Reyna was no good. They exchanged telephone numbers and told each other that each seemed like good people. Tyron told Kevin that Reyna was losing out on a good man and the conversation would be their little secret. Kevin advised Tyron that he should pay for day care, his son's clothes, buy groceries, and whatever extra activities they needed, but he shouldn't put her a dime in her hands.

The following day, Kevin decided to call Reyna to vent his frustration and to get some type of expla-nation. To his surprise, Reyna had a very bad atti-tude. She told him to fuck himself and not to ever call her again. Reyna hung up the telephone but Kevin called her back. He asked her how could she throw away their relationship so easily. Reyna responded by telling him that they never had a relationship and that she was never his woman. Once again, Kevin was in complete shock. It was hard for him to comprehend that the woman that he loved had no remorse or conscious. He felt the ultimate betrayal. Kevin was also hurt because when Larry and Reyna started working in the same building, they started asking Kevin questions periodically about on another. She admitted to Kevin that she never loved him and she just told him that to make him feel better. Reyna repeatedly told Kevin that he never had her and that he lived in a fantasy world. She also told him that he was stupid to think he was really going to get another chance. Kevin asked Reyna if she had slept with Larry and she replied, "It's none of your business." One rule on the street is if a woman says none of your business to that question that usually means that she did it. These days, a woman will be quick to say, "Hell no!" or "He didn't get shit." Women love to flaunt the idea that the person that they're dating isn't getting any. Reyna told Kevin not to ever call her again. He knew he had to leave her for good this time.

Meanwhile, Kevin wasn't able to sleep or eat for the next two days. He had been constantly throwing up and daydreaming. He told himself that he needed to get some psychiatric help because he didn't like himself at this time. He also thought about how Larry had always wanted to beat him in something, and this time he had. Although Kevin now realized that Reyna was no good, he still loved her. She was the love of his life. He had always put Reyna on a pedestal and respected and treated her like a lady. Larry had now stepped in and taken the most important person in Kevin's life. He repeatedly said aloud while crying, "You won Larry, you're a player, you're the Mac! You have mad game. Larry, you won. You took my life. I'm going through hell on earth." Larry had already slept with half of the women in the building and figured he should conquer Kevin's jewel, which he did.

Reyna was however, fools gold for Kevin. He usually went to early morning church service on Sunday, but on this particular Sunday, he was too depressed. Kevin had lost all trust in people, men and women. Actually, he felt hatred toward men because he felt that guys would throw away long-term friendships for a piece of ass. He also thought that Reyna went after the bigger car and the deeper pocket. He started to believe that Reyna would have left him for a man that made 10 cents more an hour. Kevin thought of the many ways he had visualized how to add to his income and to have a better future. He now thought women primarily concentrate on how to get money from men, rather than for themselves. Kevin had a lot of self-pity then. He even questioned God. He asked God, "Why me? I didn't deserve this." However, he knew in his spirit that God would not put more on you than you could handle.

All of Kevin's friends warned, that if Reyna paged him, he shouldn't call. Kevin watched his caller ID box so that he would know not to pick up the telephone if she did call. After a couple of days had passed, Kevin saw Reyna's name several times on the caller ID box showing repeated calls. He did not have anything to say to Reyna. He just couldn't get out of his head what she did to him. What hurt him the most was not just the fact that he saw her out with someone else, but that she was out with his friend, wearing the diamond ring that he bought her. Kevin felt that she could have at least left the ring at home, never mind the outfit and shoes that he bought and the fact that he paid to get her hair and nails done. Kevin was on the telephone later when his line beeped and it was Reyna. Kevin never clicked back over to tell the other person he wasn't coming back to finish the conversation. He immediately lashed out at Reyna, which is something he never did. He vented by telling Reyna she was dumb, that Larry had a relationship with a lady that worked with him, and he had fucked half the women in the building. Reyna told Kevin that he was lying and that Larry did not have a lady in the building and if he did, the lady was stupid. She went on to tell him that Larry wasn't his friend, according to Larry. Kevin responded that men would say anything for a piece of ass. Kevin then responded, "I guess Larry isn't friends with Chris either, right?" and Reyna said he was not.

Chris, Reyna and Kevin all worked together at one point and Reyna and Chris couldn't stand each other. Kevin even distanced himself from Chris because Reyna didn't like him. Chris and Larry would meet for lunch and trade nude magazines and porno-movies. Kevin just wasn't into that. If it didn't make dollars then it didn't make sense to Kevin. Reyna stood her ground that Chris and Larry were not friends. However, she did say Chris told Larry that he couldn't stand her. Kevin told Reyna that Chris didn't go out, that's' why you might think he and Larry aren't close. Reyna said Larry didn't like to go out either, and that he told her that he had been with a lot of women, but that was in the past. She told Kevin that Larry was still upset about him tapping on his window, and Kevin responded, "I told don't give a damn." She told Kevin that Larry also wanted her to be his woman, but she didn't want a man. At this point Kevin was disgusted, because Reyna seemed to know a little too much about Larry. Kevin and Reyna continued to argue. He told Reyna she walked out on a good man and she responded by telling Kevin he wasn't a good man. Kevin's mouth and heart just dropped when she made such a low and painful remark. Kevin really gave Reyna his all. The reason he worked two jobs was so that she wouldn't have to work so hard. He used to tell Reyna to let him take care of everything so she would not be so stressed. He took good care of her son Jason, he cooked and cleaned behind both of them. He always showered Reyna with flowers, candy, diamonds, and pearls, among many other things. If Reyna was cramping, Kevin would go to store and buy Reyna something for her pain. He almost lost his job when Reyna called him from the emergency room, because he left work immediately and neglected to tell his supervisor.

Kevin wrote Reyna poetry, rubbed her back, and massaged her feet until she fell asleep. In addition to Reyna telling Kevin he wasn't a good man, she also told him that he never loved her. Kevin told her, "I loved you with all my heart." He flashed back to a question he was once asked in a game. The question was, "If you could get in the way of a bullet to save your lady's life would you do it?" Kevin answered, "Without a doubt. I would take a bullet for Reyna and Jason." Kevin now realized that he was ready to die for Reyna and she wasn't even on his team. He told her that the one thing about crack-cocaine was that it didn't talk back to you, it couldn't sleep with somebody you know, and it couldn't tell you one minute I love you and the next minute, you're nothing." Kevin said, "Don't get me wrong, I'm against crack-cocaine, but being addicted to someone causes stress, loss of appetite, lack of sleep, and lack of concentration, which can all lead to weight loss and other health problems." The result is the same as a drug addition. Kevin asked Reyna if Larry was smoking a joint and Reyna responded, "Yeah, we were getting high." Kevin was amazed that the woman who had told him that she was against drugs admitted to getting high. He asked her how long she had been getting high, she responded that she had done it for years. She said she couldn't afford to buy it, but she would smoke it if someone else bought it. Kevin was just out-done when he realized that he had dated a pot-head.

He realized that he needed to take it one day

at a time to get Reyna out of his system. Kevin's days seemed so long without Reyna. He was in a building on the 20th floor and thought about jumping over the balcony to get it over with. He seriously thought about it, but realized Reyna was not worth dying for, and that he was too strong spiritually to kill himself. It crossed his mind to do bodily harm to Larry, but he couldn't even think about putting his hands on Reyna, because he didn't want to hurt her. Sometimes it felt like a dream, but it wasn't, it was real. Kevin was so hurt; he lashed out at one of his female friends when she asked him to pray about his situation. He said he was tired of everybody telling him to pray about it. Kevin was definitely not himself those. Two weeks had passed since Kevin had seen Reyna and Larry at the movies. He was a total mess and wasn't taking good care of himself. He needed a shave, a haircut, and he needed to wash his car. Kevin had trouble sleeping and continued to have flashbacks of the scene at the movies.

THE ROAD TO RECOVERY

It took all of Kevin's strength not to call Reyna, and it was the most difficult thing he had ever done in his life. Weeks later, Kevin was invited to his friend Greg's house for drinks and barbecue. Kevin was twenty-six and Greg was ten years older. He was at least six years younger than most of his friends. He was a very mature twenty-six year old and he didn't go out to clubs to chase women. He was somewhat of a loner, and liked the idea of family and being a provider. He wasn't always the most independent person, moving out on his own at the age of twenty. His mom paid his car insurance for him and teased him that she should be able to claim him on her taxes. He didn't like being teased about being dependent on her and eventually started paying his own car insurance. One thing Reyna drilled into Kevin's head was that he was a damn good provider. That really made Kevin feel special, like the man he always wanted to be. Kevin took great pride in helping Reyna. At that particular gathering, he really felt out of place.

Kevin sat in a corner by himself, drinking a beer, wondering what Reyna was doing, and why all this had happened to him. He thought to himself, that he must have been too boring for Reyna. Several women had told him in the past that they didn't want a relationship with him, but they would want to marry someone like him one day. Kevin was a homebody. He didn't go out to shoot pool or invite his friends over for drinks and dominoes. He was content with renting movies and cooking for his lady. He did like to go out to the movies and to dinner, but younger women liked to be in a social environment. Kevin liked to travel, but for the most part he didn't have a click that he hung out with. He was a very likeable person with a big heart. He chose to be a little more isolated with his woman than most men.

Kevin had his reasons for not liking social gatherings. When Kevin was a senior in high school, he went to a local fast food restaurant with his brother

Eric after his high school football game. He knew that it would be crowded, but he and his brother were just going to grab a bite to go. Kevin and Eric received their food and got into the jeep. Eric backed out but a group of guys where blocking the exit. One of the guys said, "Hey, they're trying to get by." Another guy shouted," Fuck them niggas'!" and Eric shouted, "Fuck you." The guy approached the jeep and hit Eric in the chest. Kevin recognized the group of guys, as the Southside Killers (a neighborhood gang). He couldn't believe what was happening. Eric jumped out of the jeep to fight and Kevin got out of the jeep to help. Kevin and Eric were both surrounded by approximately ten guys on each side. Kevin couldn't see Eric and Eric couldn't see Kevin. Kevin immediately struck one of the guys and a different one kicked at him but Kevin caught his foot and punched him in the face. Kevin was handling his own, until someone hit him in the back of the head with a weapon. He began to stagger, but never hit the ground. He fought his way into the restaurant as the gang members continuously pounded him. They were beating Kevin up on the counter near the cash registers. Kevin looked up at the manager and asked him to call the police, the manager looked at Kevin and continued to fill orders. Kevin fell into the arms of his friend John who asked Kevin if there was anything that he could do. Kevin said, "Yeah, help me get my brother." Kevin went back outside and saw the jeep leaving. He thought that maybe his brother went for help or was tearing a board off the fence or something. He went back through the other entrance to the restaurant, jumped into John's truck, and laid his head on John's girlfriend's lap so that they wouldn't follow them.

Kevin went home and called 911, which was the first call that had been received on the incident. A little later, Eric walked through the door dripping with blood and was helped inside by their Mom. Kevin asked Eric, "Where were you taking the jeep?" Eric replied, "I didn't take the jeep. They took it so that we couldn't get away." Kevin and Eric ended up with multiple injuries and hospital bills. Kevin had to transfer in the middle of the semester of his senior year to another high school because he filed a report of the incident on one of the gang members with the police. The police officer said that there was nothing that he could do and that the guy was active in Kevin's high school. They probably would just get a slap on the wrist. Kevin was warned by the police not to let anyone know where he was attending school. He wasn't even allowed to play basketball because he had to play it safe.

Although this incident happened almost ten years ago, it changed Kevin's mind about going out to clubs and certain other events where large crowds gather. It made him loose faith in the justice system and in mankind. Kevin had a relationship with a young lady during this time. When he told her about his tragic experience, she replied, "Well that's what you get for going out." He hung up the telephone in her face and never talked to her again.

PLAY IT AGAIN, KEVIN

Eric came by one Friday night and demanded that Kevin go out with him. Kevin said that he didn't want to go out but after he and Eric knocked off a twelve pack of beer, Kevin said, "Cool, I'll go out with you." They decided to go the hottest Black nightclub in town, a club called Smoothies. Smoothies was the place that all the so-called sophisticated Blacks hung out. Kevin basically walked around all night. He didn't dance or approach anyone. Everybody looked too fake to Kevin on that particular night. He saw women with price tags hanging out of their dresses, weaves hanging down their backs and most women looked overly made up. He decided to go find Eric,when he spotted him leaning up against the wall talking to two ladies. Kevin's heart felt like it would beat out of his chest. He had discovered the most beautiful woman he had seen in a while. He hadn't been that attracted to a woman since Reyna. He was very fortunate since Eric was already talking to the lady that she was with. The ladies turned out to be sisters, so Kevin and Eric had a lot in common with them. Apparently, Eric had already tried to talk to the lady that Kevin was interested in but her sister had pulled him away from her and said that she was too young for him. Kevin found out that the lady's name was Stacey and that she was only eighteen years old. The club had a restriction that you had to be at least 21 years of age to get in, but they usually let the fine women in anyway. He also found out that Stacey had a child and hadn't graduated from high school. He thought that Stacey had a very innocent look to her and that she was real young and tender. Kevin and Stacey shared a few drinks although she was below the legal drinking age. They talked, danced, and had drinks all night long. Kevin was probably the easiest guy in the club for Stacey to talk to because he wasn't stuck up and kept up with young slang and dances. He wanted to take Stacey out to breakfast, but Eric didn't want to because he didn't hit it off with her sister. Eric had driven, and had seen Sarah, his chidren's mother, in the club with another guy, so he was aggravated about that. Kevin ended up walking Stacey to her car where they exchanged telephone numbers. He was so excited about Stacey that he only vaguely heard his brother's dilemma with Sarah. Kevin called Stacey when he got home, but she was already asleep. He called Stacey every day for a month and was never able to contact her. He even left messages begging for her to call. Finally, he decided to just give up.

IS THAT YOU CINDERELLA?

One afternoon he went by his mom's house for a short visit. His mom asked him to go to the grocery store to get her prescription filled. He didn't feel like going because he was depressed. Some of his depression was because he had looked forward to getting to know Stacey, but it didn't work out. As Kevin walked around the store waiting for the prescription to be filled, he saw a beautiful woman walk right by him. He didn't get to make eye contact with her but the woman was so pretty that he had to go back and do a double take. He went back to see who this mystery woman was and to his surprise, it was Stacey. He couldn't do anything but smile. As he approached her it was obvious that she was surprised to see him. He told her how he had been trying to contact her and she responded, "You couldn't have." He quoted her telephone number from memory and Stacey was impressed. She gave him another number to contact her and he gave her his number because Stacey claimed that she had lost his telephone number the night they met. He dropped off the prescription at his mother's house and went back home to check his messages. He had one from Stacey asking him to call her at his convenience. He was ecstatic to know that he might have an opportunity to get to know his Cinderella. Kevin immediately called Stacey. She told him that he had her sister's phone number and that she didn't live with her sister. She also told Kevin that her sister never told her that he had called. They made plans for a date on that following Saturday and talked each day leading up to Saturday. Stacey was in the process of moving back home with her parents. Kevin was curious as to how an eighteen-year old girl with a child was keeping an apartment without a job but he didn't think it was any of his business as long as he wasn't paying her bills. He took Stacey to dinner and a concert and they had a ball. He liked the idea that Stacey would ask him a lot of questions as if she looked up to him. He loved Stacey's innocent eyes and her smile almost looked as if she had never been touched. He asked her about her child's father and Stacey told him that he made her feel ugly. Kevin couldn't believe that a woman so beautiful could have such low self-esteem. All of a sudden, he felt a lot closer to Stacey. He couldn't believe that they had so much in common. He was really trying to lift his own self-esteem after his break up with Reyna. Kevin told Stacey that it was good that she made mistakes in her relationships while she was young. He told her that it was hard to deal with being an old fool, because by his age he should know better. He told Stacey that if she need-ed a friend, he would be there for her because the world was too big and evil to try to figure it out on your own. He took Stacey home, walked her to the door and gave her a good bye hug. He really wanted to kiss Stacey, but Kevin was old fashioned. He called Stacey when he got home and said, "I really enjoyed myself tonight," and Stacey responded, "Likewise." Kevin and Stacey began to go out every weekend for a month and things started to get serious. He really loved to cook for his woman and he could cook better than the majority of the women he dated. He could cook anything that you wanted to eat. Once he cooked for you, you would want him to cook for you all the time. He had Stacey so addicted to his cook-ing, and his sense of humor, that eventually she start-ed coming over every day. Stacey felt good inside because she had not been able to laugh for months.

He was happy to entertain a beautiful woman who looked up to him and found his jokes funny. Kevin and Stacey made love after dating for a month and a half. He tried before that, but Stacey wouldn't let him. Sex had become a big joke to Stacey and Kevin because Kevin hadn't had sex in a while and he was very horny. He never forced himself upon Stacey because he wanted their first time to be special. It didn't quite work out as planned. They had sex right there on Kevin's living room couch. They decided to become a couple, which seemed like something that both of them really wanted. He liked Stacey because she would come over and drink with him and they would laugh together a lot. Kevin also liked the fact that Stacey lived with her parents and didn't ever seem to need money from him. She often invited him out for dinner or the movies and paid the bill. That was a real change for Kevin. She just seemed so appreciative of whatever Kevin did for her. He really admired that quality, plus Stacey looked up to him. He and Stacey were having the time of their lives and both felt their relationship was a blessing from God. Stacey's family was very fond of Kevin and vice-versa. He and Stacey shared their wicked past lives exchanging horror stories, but agreeing how they went from 'rags to riches.' His answering machine now said, "The only important message is from Stacey, so everybody else just hang up." He couldn't believe that a woman so much younger could make him so happy. Kevin and Stacey started exchanging gifts at random and he found out what it was like to be in a relationship that's 50-50. Once again, Kevin believed that he had found his soul mate. He also became very close to Stacey's child Lamar, who had just made a year old. Kevin wanted a child really bad, but he wanted to do it the right way.

Kevin was always very good with kids. He came from a big family, and his mother kept foster children, so Kevin had a lot of experience with children. One of Kevin's most important goals was to become a father, but he hadn't been that lucky yet. Kevin had given up on the idea of finding Miss Right. Although he came from a Christian family, he said if he ever found a woman, who would treat him right, he would have a child out of wedlock. Kevin took to Lamar as if he were his own son, and Lamar adored him. Kevin just couldn't believe how happy he was. Although Stacey hadn't finished high school and didn't seem very ambitious, Kevin was content with that. He never really cared how well a woman was doing as far as her career goes, because he felt that if he took care of business as far as his career went, they would both be okay. He believed that if two people are genuinely happy together, it didn't matter what material lifestyle they had, what matters was how they treated each other. Kevin had witnessed plenty of people from low-income families doing very well and happy with each other even though they lacked many material things. Kevin had also witnessed people that were financially well off or even famous end their relationship in divorce. Money was important to Kevin, but happiness was equally important. He knew he was very happy with Stacey. She seemed to be maturing with each passing day since she started dating Kevin. Even though Kevin and Stacey met at a club, neither one of them had been back since they met. It seemed like such a long time, since Kevin and Stacey experienced any pain. They were both so happy, it was hard to remember all the pain that they had suffered in the past.

THE NEXT LEVEL

Kevin loved to buy Stacey flowers and Kevin would buy roses every week. Kevin and Stacey weren't only partners, but they were best friends. Kevin and Stacey shared some of their most intimate secrets, with each other. Kevin decided it was time to buy Stacey a ring that he spent a small fortune on. A month after Kevin bought Stacey the ring, she missed her period and suspected she was pregnant, so they bought a home pregnancy test. Stacey took the test, showed it to Kevin with a smirk on her face. Kevin thought that meant she wasn't pregnant, but she was. He gave her a big hug and kiss and told her not to worry about anything. He took on another full-time job, which meant he was working sixteen hours a day to save money. He opened a joint bank account with Stacey and told her he would deposit his entire check from the second job in the account so she could take whatever she needed. He also bought some parenting books to read on his lunch breaks. He wanted to learn everything he possibly could to be the best father he could be. Kevin and Stacey discussed baby names on a daily basis. He began to take Stacey to prayer meetings so that they could become closer to God. He was so concerned with her diet that he would find time to cook the night before and have her lunch prepared for the next day. He told Stacey that he wanted to have the baby with her, and he wanted to feel her pain. He told her not to worry about any-thing, and if she had a problem he would solve it. This was so different for Stacey, considering Lamar's father was very insensitive during her pregnancy. Kevin hired a nanny to take care of Lamar when Stacey was only two months pregnant. He told his friends his time had arrived and that he finally had a winning lady on his team. He came home every day from a hard day's work looking forward to rubbing Stacey's feet and fixing her a hot meal. He was defi-nitely one of a kind.

Kevin and Stacey were still trying to decide on a name. He asked Stacey if it would be okay if the child was a boy to make him a junior. Stacey had a peculiar look on her face and said that, she had given her ex a junior, and if it were a boy, she would like to name it after her deceased father. Kevin couldn't help but understand her feelings. He said, "I don't care what the child's name is, I just hope we are blessed with a healthy baby. I will give our baby all the love that it needs." She told him that she couldn't think of a better person to go through her pregnancy with than him. Kevin was always there for Stacey and he couldn't be happier. He admitted that he didn't think that he could produce children for some reason.

Reyna would often tell Kevin when they argued that he couldn't produce a child. She knew that Kevin desperately wanted a child of his own and this was her way of hitting below the belt. He never really tried to have a child out of wedlock because he wanted to do things the right way. Reyna however, put some doubts in Kevin's head. She would tell him that he was going to be shooting blanks his whole life and would never experience a child's birth. In spite of Reyna's prediction, he had a special feeling in the back of his mind, that Reyna didn't know what she was talking about. He began to stick his chest out again and felt as manly as ever. He wanted to be the best father he could be because he loved Stacey, and furthermore, he loved the idea of having a child. He decided to do some volunteer work at a local nursery to get even more experience with babies. Kevin had a lot of experience with kids because he was in a program where he was a mentor for several young juvenile boys. He would take these troubled teens with absent fathers to pro baseball games, basketball games and barbecues. He would also tutor these guys in school, to do his part for the community. He really had a big heart and deserved everything positive that was happening to him.

MY BED

Can I please go to sleep?

No, I can't sleep knowing my mate is at home

laying in between the sheets; where I usually lay.

But on this day, someone else is in my place.

Man, I wish that I could sleep, but I toss and turn

wondering to myself, when will I learn?

Why do I do this? Take the pain,

is it because I'm in love or am I just insane.

I don't know. What should I do?

This is stress; I can't take the mental abuse.

I know one thing, I don't need this;

I deserve better,

so I have decided to get out of this.

CHAPTER IV

Age Ain't Nothing But A Number

Steve was one year away from graduating from high school, and had a job working for the county. He was doing well. He had his own car and place at seventeen in the eleventh grade. One day Steve observed two young ladies entering the building where he worked. One of the ladies casually approached Steve and introduced herself and her sister Evonne. She asked Steve if he had a girlfriend, and he replied, "No, I don't." The young lady proceeded to explain to Steve that her sister, Evonne, found him to be very attractive and wanted to know if he'd be interested in exchanging telephone numbers. Steve glanced over at Evonne and said, "Sure." He also found Evonne to be very beautiful. He wondered why a sister with skin the color of caramel and a figure like Halle Berry would need to be "hooked up." Whatever the reason may have been, Steve was just elated that he "was the Man." Evonne called Steve the very next day. They engaged in casual conversation in which Evonne revealed to Steve that she was twenty-four years old and was a single parent of a six-year old daughter. Steve asked Evonne if the fact that he was only seventeen would hinder his chance of getting to know her better. She answered, "Normally it would, but you have more going for yourself than some of the older men that I have dated." Evonne told Steve that she didn't have a guy in her life. She had been dating a couple of men, however, when she lost her job, got her phone disconnected and her lights turned off, neither guy offered to help. She continued to explain that when she got her new phone number, she decided that no one from her past would have it. She also said that she had only had her new telephone connected for one week, and no other man had the number. He asked Evonne to give him a chance to show her what kind of man he was, and if she didn't like what he had to offer, they could just go their separate ways. If she did like Steve, there would be no excuse for another man ever getting her phone number or her time. Evonne told him that she liked the sound of that and would take him up on his offer. Steve and Evonne saw each other every day, partly because Evonne didn't have her own means of transportation. Steve took Evonne and her daughter back and forth from her mother's house to Evonne's house. Evonne was unemployed at the time and lacked any type of marketable skill. Steve spent a couple of hours each day teaching her typing and basic word processing skills. He also typed her resume and worked with her on numerous other computer applications. His hard work eventually paid off. A friend of his, who was an office manager at a prominent company, gave Evonne a job as an Administrative

Assistant. Evonne and Steve still did not have a serious relationship, however, they had been intimate on
a couple of occasions.

Steve and Evonne would take turns spending
the night at each other's house. He became very
close to Evonne's family. He was so close in fact,
Evonne's mother started calling him "son-in-law."
Steve knew the relationship was growing, and was
very content that it was. Steve noticed the kinds of
food Evonne and her daughter liked eating and
included them in his grocery list so that when they
came over to eat, they would feel that much more at
home.

Steve was a very busy man. He worked from
4 p.m. to midnight, and went to school from eight in
the morning until noon, so there wasn't much time for
rest. He got a disturbing call from Evonne one night
when he returned home from work. She called from
the hospital, after she, and her sister had been
involved in an automobile accident in her mom's car.
He looked at the clock, which reflected 2 a.m. Despite
the fact that he was deliriously exhausted and also
had to take an anatomy exam in just a few hours, he
drug himself out of bed to go to the hospital to check
on Evonne. He waited at the hospital until 5 a.m.
before she was finally released. She appeared to be
okay other than being a little sore. He took Evonne
and her sister home. Steve bought Evonne a bottle of
body rub lotion and a heating pad for her sore mus-
cles. He went to the grocery store to buy something
to cook for Evonne and to pick up a few items for him-

self. Since he knew Evonne was a tidy person, he cleaned her apartment, washed her clothes, and then gave her a massage. He even cooked Evonne a big breakfast, before he left. As he got ready to leave for school, he asked Evonne if she would rather him stay with her, and she said, "Yes." He told her that he could always take anatomy next semester.

Steve ended up running late for work trying to take care of Evonne, but he promised to call her as soon as he got to work. Steve made it to his job and called Evonne, and a man answered the phone. Steve told him that he must have dialed the wrong number and hung up. He tried calling again for Evonne and the strange man answered once more. Steve asked to speak to Evonne and the man said hold on and put Evonne on the phone. Steve asked, "Is that your Uncle Fred?" Evonne replied, "No." Steve asked, "Is that your cousin Walt?" and Evonne said, " No, he's a friend." Steve couldn't believe it. He had just left twenty minutes ago. What was that guy doing, watching to see when he left? Steve told Evonne, "Well, I was just calling to check on you." Steve thought to himself, "Damn! Why didn't she have him pick her up from the hospital? I could have been getting some rest and preparing for my anatomy test."

Steve never told Evonne how he felt, however, he started to see other people, and began talking to Evonne as nothing more than another homegirl.

Evonne had the hots for Steve, and constantly tried to get with him, but she didn't understand why he wasn't interested anymore. Steve lost major respect for Evonne, but because they were friends and he was so cool with her family, he didn't cut her totally off. Evonne got very upset with Steve when Valentine's Day came around and Steve didn't even get her a card. He told Evonne that she wasn't his Valentine and asked her if she got him anything. She told him that she didn't get him anything, so Steve told her to call the guy who answered her phone that day he called from work. Evonne said, "I knew something was bugging you, but I didn't know what." Still, Evonne didn't offer any explanation, and Steve didn't have to hear about Valentine's Day anymore. Steve and Evonne are friends to this day, and Evonne definitely wants to marry Steve, but he is totally not interested.

A Blast From The Past!

Kevin received a strange call at his new place of employment. He answered the phone and some woman just yelled out, "You're a sorry, punk ass, trick bitch!" and hung up in his face. Kevin recognized the voice as Reyna's. He was puzzled as he wondered how Reyna got his new work number and why she would call to curse him. He called Reyna to ask her not to call him at his new job anymore, when she began to tell him how happy she was without him. She started telling Kevin about some guy who played professional football for their hometown team last year, played with another NFL team for three years, who had a huge home, and drove a Lexus. She then told Kevin the guy's name, and Kevin didn't recognize it, which was strange to him because he used to write sports articles for his home team. She told him about another guy named Larry and all he had going for himself. She bragged to Kevin that she had two good men and that he should try to get to where they already were. Kevin told Reyna that he was happy for her, but he now had a woman in his life that makes him very happy, and he thought it was disrespectful to her if they continued their conversation. Kevin said, "Please don't call me anymore," and Reyna replied, "Fuck you! You're just mad because you couldn't afford me." Kevin said, "Goodbye, Reyna," and hung up the phone. He called his cousin John to tell him what had just happened, and John told him that Reyna was out there pretty bad. He asked John to elaborate, and John told Kevin about a birthday party that his daughter attended. Reyna was also at the party. She came in and said things like, "Girl, I haven't even been home to change clothes yet." She had spent the night with some guy and they had been intimate all night long. Then Reyna went on to say, "Let me page Larry, he's been so good to me." Shortly thereafter, Larry showed up to join her at the birthday party. John asked Kevin, "Are you hurt by this even though you have a lady with a baby on the way?" Kevin said, "I guess what bothers me is that it took me such a long time to get over her. I mean, I went through a period of mourning and she didn't mourn at all because she was fucking around while we were together. It hurts to know it's like she never cared." Kevin also said that he finally realized that Reyna brought nothing to the relationship. He told John how he had financed the relationship and always went out of his way to make her feel special. He went on to explain, "Reyna is a very beautiful lady, but she thinks men are supposed to treat her like a queen. She expects her bills to be paid and everything, but she never does anything to make her man feel special." He said that Black men need to get out of the "trophy phase" where they are so concerned with how a sister looks that they'll settle for less and put up with just about anything. He told John that Black men, should start looking at sisters that are slightly overweight, or have other physical flaws, because there are very special women who often get passed up. "Some Black men also have a color complex," he said, "They think that anything closer to white is right. We need to start looking at the inside of a person to see if they can make us happy mentally, even before we get caught up with the physical aspects. It's a crying shame that scandalous women like Reyna, with nothing to offer, get all the good men, and some wonderful sister with more to offer sits at home because we didn't find her as pretty." Kevin asked John to hold on a moment. When he came back, he told John that the guy Reyna was dating wasn't on any NFL team and never played pro football. John told Kevin that he must have been doing something if he had a nice house and a Lexus. Kevin replied, "Yeah, he's probably a drug dealer." John said, "Man, stop player-hating!" "I guess you're right," Kevin replied, "But I still feel sorry for her son Jason. You know what John? I think this would really upset me if I didn't have a wonderful woman at home. I mean, seriously, Stacey has shown me what a real woman is all about. I'm her king and she's my queen! I can't express how happy I am to be in a give-and-take relationship instead of just giving all the time. If those other brothers are wise, they'll eventually want someone who can bring something to the relationship other than a fat ass. That's probably why Reyna never keeps anyone. She probably burns them out because brothers do get tired of dependents." As Kevin got off the phone, he said, "Well, anyway, I have to go before I lose my job."

Bitter Sweet Success

It was Kevin's lucky year. He got a job offer for an exclusive position in another state. Kevin had applied with a particular company every year for the past four years, but never got an offer. The position Kevin applied for involved an executive training program. Kevin could increase his income by fifteen thousand dollars in the first year. The company gave Kevin three weeks to reply to their offer. He was very excited and knew that this couldn't have happened at a better time since he was expecting his first child. He decided to invite Stacey over for a candlelight dinner. He prepared lobster, grilled shrimp, tossed salad, and French bread. Kevin also went out and spent two hundred-dollars for a bottle of champagne. Kevin called Stacey and told her to do whatever it was she needed to do, but to be at his place at 7 p.m. Stacey asked why, but Kevin didn't tell her anything except that it concerned their future. Stacey continued to beg Kevin to tell her, but he was strong and withheld the good news. Jokingly, Stacey said, "Alright, but don't make me hurt you." She came over and the candlelight dinner almost brought tears to her eyes. Kevin told Stacey about the job offer. She asked Kevin if that was the company that he had been dreaming to work with since high school, and he said yes as he ran up to give her a big hug and kiss. But to his dismay, Stacey pulled back and said, "I can't believe you!" With a puzzled look on his face, Kevin said, "What?" Stacey replied, "I can't believe you're going to leave your woman and child in another state." Kevin responded, "I'm not!" Stacey told Kevin that she wouldn't move out of Texas because all of her family and friends were there. "What do I look like following you to another state with two kids? And what am I supposed to do if you get up there and start acting like a fool or something?" "Acting a fool? Explain this to me Stacey." She said, "Like not coming home or getting abusive or something. I wouldn't have anywhere to go." Kevin was shocked as he asked if he had ever shown any signs of such behavior, and Stacey replied, "No, but most men don't until they think they have you in the middle of nowhere with no friends." Kevin said, "Stacey, I love you, I love Lamar, and I love our child to be. I would never do anything like that. I want to do right by God, to continue to get the blessings I got when you and Lamar came into my life." Stacey said, "I'm not ready to marry you yet; I'm still too young." Kevin replied reluctantly, "Well, I respect you and myself too much to shack up." Stacey agreed. Kevin asked Stacey if she loved him, and she answered, "With all my heart." Kevin told her that he wanted to spend the rest of his life with her and only her and asked if she felt the same way. She replied, "Of course I do." "Well, make me a happy man and marry me." Kevin responded. Stacey told him she couldn't do that just yet, so Kevin asked what the next step would be. Stacey paused and said; "Well I guess you'll just run off from me like all the other men in my past." Kevin said, "Run off from you? I would never do that!" They both paused, then Stacey began to wipe away her own tears as she said, "I'll miss you, Kevin, and so will your baby." Kevin was confused. "Miss me how?" he asked. She shouted, "When you leave!" "Let me tell you some- thing," Kevin said, "If you still won't go with me, then fuck that job. There will be other jobs, but there's only one special woman for me. Maybe one day I'll get another chance at the job when you are ready to marry me. And who's to say that I won't get a job right here in town that's just as good?" Kevin put his arm around Stacey and said, "You are my everything, and you come first right now." Stacey looked up at Kevin and said, "Right now?" Kevin said, "That's right, until the baby is born, you come first. After that, I'll have two babies!" Stacey kissed Kevin and told him how much she loved him. She then told him that she needed to get home before it got too late. Kevin said, "Okay, let me walk you to your car, baby." Kevin kissed Stacey good night and told her that the company would get his answer the next day.

The Big Fishing Expedition

It was time for Reyna, Yolanda, and Michelle to go to the club to get some new clients. The girls prepared for the experience a whole week in advance. During the course of the week, they dieted and worked out. The girls got one of their male friends to buy them a new outfit and another male friend to pay to get their hair, nails, and feet done. They usually kept at least three steady companions, and every now and then, if they got lucky, one of the male friends might get to meet with them for breakfast. It was showtime, and the girls looked great, except for their tendency to all wear the same hairstyle. They usually wear whatever style Reyna got, which didn't show a whole lot of individuality. They got to the club, and the guys were all over them like white on rice. The girls would only give a guy the time of day if they were talking about money or offering to buy them drinks. They didn't turn down any free drinks, and the drinks just kept coming. This was the ladies lucky day, because Reyna and Yolanda met drug dealers, and Michelle met a popular NBA player. This was cool because Michelle could hook the other girls up with some of the basketball player's teammates, and Reyna and Yolanda could hook Michelle up with their drug dealers' buddies. They all went out to breakfast with their new clients. These guys actually have more money than all the guys they have been dating do. That meant that one or maybe two of their present clients might get dropped so they could put more emphasis on the new client. The old clients did their jobs by supplying the ladies with everything they need to attract the new clients. That's the way it goes in their business. A guy does not have any job security, in one day, and out the next. The business constantly changed faces as time passed.

Timing couldn't have been any better for Michelle. She got the prize of all prizes when she caught a NBA man. His name was Chris and he was "The Man". He was tall, handsome, and rich. You should have seen how many women were all over Chris when he went out, and he was on just as many women as the ones on him. Chris was what you would call a "hoe"! Everyone that knew anyone knew someone that he had slept with at one time or another. Chris was one of those brothers who had about fifty women thinking that he was their man. They knew he was wild, but Chris had skills. He told women that because of the public spotlight he was in, he couldn't be seen with them often. Chris told them that the tabloid photographers hid in his bushes, waiting for him to go somewhere in public, and tried to catch him doing anything out of the ordinary. He told them that he didn't want his woman under a microscope like that until it was inevitable, and it would be inevitable once they got married. Heck, that was all Chris had to tell Michelle since she was married anyway. Chris would throw these wild parties with all his ladies and that would make them feel special, because he would have some of his cooler relatives over as well. The ladies would feel special because Chris would invite them to the party and introduce them to his relatives. Little did they know that he was dating seventy-five percent of the guests. What was so cool was that none of them would sweat him because of the line about being in the spotlight and wanting to keep their relationship private. Chris also had two phone lines in his house. One was a personal line, and the other was for business. He would turn the ringer off on his personal phone when he had company, and let the ladies answer his business line. No one had his business number other than people that paid him or people that he paid. That really made the women feel like they were the only one.

Michelle started telling her friends that it was time to get some of his money. She approached Chris about money and he told her that he would put her on his personal payroll as a tax write-off. He told Michelle that he would give her one thousand dollars a month to be his personal love slave. Chris said, "Hey, I'll just tell them you're my personal massage therapist." Michelle thought to herself, "I hope he's serious, because that is over half my salary for a month." That would be the push she needed to get over the thirty thousand dollar a year mark, and hell, it would just be crumbs to Chris because he brought home about one hundred and sixty thousand a month. The deal that Chris offered Michelle was a deal fifteen other women already had. Michelle and Chris began to have protected sex, however, Michelle thought that if she could get pregnant by Chris, he would have to pay her a large amount of hush-up money. For her to agree to have an abortion, he would give her a huge sum of money so he wouldn't have to pay child support.

Even though Michelle was married, she knew she could get a divorce upon getting pregnant, and Chris would have to pay so much in child support that it would be more than her and her husband's salary combined. One day while Chris was in the restroom preparing to have sex with Michelle, she reached for the condom and got a small needle from her purse. She began to punch small holes in the center of the condom. She was so involved into her little scheme that she didn't even notice that Chris had entered the room and was standing right over her head. With a perplexed and somewhat distorted look on his face, Chris asked, "What the hell are you doing?" She replied, "Nothing," as she tried to hide the condom. Chris reached behind her back, forced her hand open, and saw the needle and condom. He said, "Michelle, if you wanted to have unprotected sex, all you needed to do was tell me. Hell, I hate using condoms anyway! I was only using them for your benefit out of respect the fact that you are married and you probably didn't want to take a chance on having another man's child other than your husband's." Michelle told him that she didn't care about that, but went on to ask him if he had unprotected sex with all the women he slept with. Chris replied, "You might think I'm crazy, but if it's your time to go, then it's your time to go. So to be honest, I never use condoms." Michelle replied, "You don't use a condom with any of the women you sleep with." "Yep," replied Chris, "I don't just sleep with whores, I sleep with women like you who have basically been with one man. Besides, groupies won't fuck just anybody; they strictly fuck people who are somebody. It's not that often that they get with too many famous people, so actually, groupies have less sex than everybody else." Michelle said, "That is interesting, but anyone with any common sense knows that you can get sexually transmitted diseases from any category of people."

After all that discussion, Michelle and Chris still had unprotected sex for several months. Chris would even fly Michelle out to some of his games every now and then, which would make her feel extra special. Michelle, however, did not realize that Chris had his ladies on a rotating schedule. There are ninety NBA games a year including exhibitions, and not including the playoffs, so Michelle was one of many who all felt like the only one.

End Of The Road

It was time for the annual blood drive that was sponsored by Michelle's employer. Michelle always donated a pint of blood each year. She donated her pint, got a free T-shirt, and went on her merry way. A few days later, she received a letter in the mail from the hospital that said she needed to come in for an interview regarding her blood test. Michelle's husband opened the letter and read it before she got home, and told her about it as she came in. Michelle thought it was it's no big deal since her blood type, "A Positive," was so rare. She assumed that the hospital wanted her to donate more blood. Surprisingly to her, Michelle's husband said that he was going to the hospital with her and wanted to sit in on the interview. Michelle and her husband fought all the way to the hospital. Michelle told her husband that he was making her nervous, so he agreed to sit in the waiting room. While Michelle was in her interview, her husband went through her purse and found a letter and checks from Chris. He was furious, but decided to keep his cool.

The doctor asked Michelle to have a seat. He just came right out and informed Michelle that her blood tested HIV positive. The doctor asked her who she had been sleeping with, and she told him that it was none of his business. The doctor and Michelle continued to talk for about ten more minutes as he explained the implication of the disease. As Michelle walked out of the office crying, her husband said, "I'll

bet you have AIDS, you no-good tramp. I read the letter from your NBA boyfriend, and saw how happy he
was that you're not having protected sex anymore.
Well you can just walk home, or have him come pick
you up, and you'd better hope I don't have that shit,
because I'll kill your ass, bitch!" He continued angrily,
"Oh, and just forget about seeing the kids. They don't
need to be around an infected, dirty-ass slut!"
Michelle got Yolanda to come pick her up and she
made Yolanda swear not to tell anyone, and Yolanda
swore. Yolanda had every intention of keeping
Michelle's secret but, you know how it is when you
hear something tragic, and you have to tell one person, and they have to tell one person, and so on.

That one person that Yolanda told was Reyna,
and Reyna told one person, and by mid-afternoon
Monday, everyone in the office knew that Michelle
was HIV positive. The news got back to Michelle
through this guy named Howard who had been trying
to get with Michelle for about a year. Howard confronted Michelle after work and said, "That's what you
get for always calling me a broke ass nigga'."
Confused, Michelle asked, "What do I get?" "AIDS
you stupid bitch! Everyone knows," replied Howard.
Michelle decided she couldn't go to work anymore
and never spoke to Yolanda and Reyna again.
Michelle called Chris to tell him about the test results.
Needless to say, Chris hung up in her face and put a
block on her calls. Chris sounded as if he knew where
she had gotten the disease. She tried to cash the last
check she had received from Chris, but he had

stopped payment on it. Michelle's life was in an uproar, with no friends, no husband, no kids, no job, no car, and no money. She decided to stay locked in the house for a while and wanted to see if her luck would change.

Living The Life

Yolanda really had it going on with Bookie, the drug dealer she met at the club. Bookie made Yolanda his main lady. In fact, Bookie didn't mess around a whole lot. He usually kept one main lady, but every now and then, he would screw somebody on the down low. But he was always true to his workers and his friends. Bookie really s liked Yolanda, she was his lady. He would let Yolanda drive any of his eight cars, and she had the keys to two of his houses. Bookie would give Yolanda eight or nine hundred dollars a month just to go shopping. Yolanda didn't even have to ask him for money. He would just reach into his pocket and say, "Here's a little something for you to line your pockets with." He also took care of Yolanda's kids. They didn't have a need for anything. Yolanda had finally met a man she could brag on. Now, Yolanda was crazy-sexy-cool. She rode around in fancy cars with chrome rims and booming sound systems. She had the fresh clothes and the cash to go with them. She was on top of the world, because she went from the lady her friends used to laugh at to the lady they bragged about. Bookie wanted Yolanda to stop working, because he didn't have very busy days.

She compromised with him by missing a lot of days from work, but in her mind, she still felt that she needed to keep a job. You have to understand the new game on the streets: make your man take care of you, but keep your job for security. If they rely on a man too much, the brother might get too controlling. These women didn't want a brother to have an edge, and that's why Yolanda wouldn't give up her job. She liked to sleep in late, give her man a little sex, and cap it off by going to the mall. This lifestyle was kind of different for Yolanda because she usually didn't pick her men by how much money they had. She had never dated a drug dealer, but she was tired of being teased by her friends. Dating Bookie was like living on the edge for Yolanda because she normally didn't find guys like that attractive. She had the attitude that Bookie had been dealing for ten years and hadn't gotten caught, plus he wasn't your average drug dealer. If you asked Yolanda, "Bookie is very smart. He has his own businesses, he goes to church, and as far as I'm concerned, he's a good man," she would always say. Yolanda was rationalizing dating Bookie. Besides, Bookie was good to everybody. Sometimes he would even give Yolanda's friends a couple of hundred dollars to go shopping with her, because they would joke about being tired of watching Yolanda shop when all they could do was window shop. So, Yolanda couldn't break up with Bookie even if she had wanted to. Bookie had money coming out of the "GaZoo."

One Saturday night, Yolanda and Bookie decided to go to the club and they both had a little buzz. On the way home, Yolanda asked Bookie to drop the top on the convertible so she could get some air, or so she could throw up if need be. He granted her request and let the top down. Bookie pulled up to a light about two miles away from the club when some guys in a white Cadillac rushed past his car while firing several shots. He wasn't hit, but unfortunately Yolanda was shot in the neck. Bookie frantically rushed her to the hospital as he sped off. Yolanda was in critical condition after undergoing eight hours of surgery, she now talks through a voice box. She had to miss several weeks from work because of the accident. Since she had already missed so many days prior to the accident, she lost her job, and contemplated whether or not to stay with Bookie. Meanwhile, Bookie didn't seem as interested in Yolanda after she had been shot.

Who's Playing Who?

Reyna didn't invest a lot of time in the drug dealer she met at the club. She already had her hands full with two guys she was seriously dating and her child's father, who she occasionally dated. The guy Reyna met at the club was named Tuggie, but everyone called him Big-T, and Reyna called him Tug. Tug had been sweating Reyna like crazy, and she would spend some time with him, but there just weren't enough hours in the day. As time went on, Reyna began to think of all the money Yolanda got from Bookie, so she decided to give Tug a chance. She felt like she learned a valuable lesson from Yolanda, never spend too much time with a drug dealer, and never ride in his car unless it's broad daylight and on the good side of town. Reyna began to meet Tug for drinks, and sometimes they met for a nice lunch. They shared daily conversations over the telephone and went out six or seven times. Tug never tried to kiss Reyna, or hold her hand, and not one time did he mention sex to her. She was beginning to think that he was different from the negative stereotype of drug dealers. Reyna began to tell everyone what a gentleman Tug was, and she thought all he wanted was her ear to listen to him. She also liked Tug because she could tell him about the other guys she dated and he didn't get upset, better yet, he could carry on a pleasant conversation about it. Reyna couldn't stand jealous men. That was one of the main reasons she knew she couldn't be with Kevin.

Tug started giving Reyna money. He would even meet her at the mall, buy her a few things, and then they would go their separate ways. To Reyna, Tug was the perfect "Trick." She was getting paid and he hadn't seen her home and she hadn't seen his. Furthermore, he still hadn't even held her hand, so Reyna, felt that she was getting over like a fat rat. She began bragging to everyone about how he bought her this and that and hadn't even come close to sleeping with her.

In the streets, a man tries to get as much sex as he can, while putting out as little money as possible, and a woman tries to get as much money as she can with as little sex as possible. That's how you tally the score. But when a woman is getting a lot of money from a man, and not putting out, it's like pitching a shut out in baseball or hitting it big at the Black Jack tables. Reyna had the perfect game plan. Tug seemed to be just as content as he wanted to be just by being in the presence of a beautiful woman.

Reyna began having so much fun taking Tug's money that she would page him with a 911 when she needed some, and he would call back talking like he was obligated to give her cash. Reyna was at the top of her game, and no one could quite figure out Big-T. What was Tug's angle? Who wanted to just give out free money? But you know what they say in the hood, "See a fool, use a fool!"

One Friday evening, Reyna was at home alone, because Jason's father had him for the weekend. Reyna promised Tug that she would meet him for a drink, but she was exhausted. Tug was cool with the fact that Reyna was tired, but she heard the disappointment in his voice. Reyna did something she had never done before, and told Tug he could stop by if he picked up some Chinese food. Reyna gave him the directions to her apartment, and Tug came over with the Chinese food and a bottle of wine. They ate and got a buzz from the wine. Tug started to massage Reyna's feet and body until she really felt relaxed. He began to kiss Reyna and she allowed him to do so. Out of curiosity, Reyna reached over and stroked Tug's penis to get a quick measurement.

After that, Tug got very aggressive and begged Reyna to let him taste her intimate areas. Reyna said, "Okay, but that's it. We not having intercourse." She couldn't help but think about what happened to her girl Michelle and the HIV, and besides, she was already sleeping with three men whose sexual history she felt she knew. Tug began to explore Reyna beneath her navel with his tongue but Reyna didn't think that he was doing a good job. She told Tug to just stop but he continued on with his mission. She grabbed the sides of Tug's cheeks and made eye contact with him as she told him again to stop in a firmer tone. He didn't say anything; instead he climbed on top of her and forced himself inside of her. There was nothing Reyna could do at that point, because Tug was about six foot five and weighed about two hundred and sixty pounds. Reyna scratched and clawed, but Tug continued to pound away in a fit of fury. He eventually stopped after about twenty minutes. It seemed like twenty hours to Reyna who cried the whole time. Tug got up and walked out. Meanwhile, Reyna realized that she didn't know Tug's real name or where he lived. She was afraid that if she called the police to report the incident, it would only humiliate her even more. The last thing she wanted was for the other guys she fooled around with to find out she was involved in a date rape, because according to Reyna, that was the only kind of rape. She did however, get Yolanda to call Bookie to try to find out where Tug lived because she wanted to have him set up. Since Bookie and

Yolanda hadn't been the same since Yolanda got shot, Bookie pretended not to know where his friend was or where he lived.

Reyna didn't want to have sex for a while, but was too afraid to show her clients any change in her personality. She began to throw up in the bathroom every time she had sex for the next six months. The incident with Tug was a learning experience for her. She should have known that you don't get something for nothing. The game she thought she was winning over Tug by so many points all of a sudden felt like a come back loss.

HEARTBREAKER!

She goes for the jugular and drains you dry.

When you have nothing left, she says goodbye.

Now it's time for her to prey

on another man that she thinks will pay.

Not caring about your feelings or your heart.

You're just another victim that she tore apart.

Too bad, so sad is what she said. She thinks you're

weak because you cared.

Well I guess she's right, how could you have

feelings for such a nothing, low life.

CHAPTER V

The New Arrival

Kevin was on his way home from work at around 7 p.m. on a Friday evening. He went home to change clothes and made it to Stacey's house at about 9 o'clock. As soon as Kevin stepped into the house, Stacey's sister ran to him explaining that Stacey's water had just broken, Kevin immediately stepped into action and helped Stacey to his car. Kevin was extremely nervous and broke out into a sweat on the way to the hospital. Once they made it to the hospital, he got Stacey settled in, then he called all his friends and family, who arrived shortly thereafter. At about 3 a.m., Kevin witnessed his first child being born. Chills came over his body as the doctor passed him the seven pound, nine ounce, seventeen inch long baby boy. Kevin's tears of joy began to flow as he dropped to his knees and thanked God for delivering a healthy child with no complications during childbirth for Stacey. Kevin went back to the waiting room and announced the birth of his son. He gave everyone a hug and kiss, then passed out cigars. Kevin told everyone how nervous he had been and that this day had turned out to be the best day of his life. He also told everyone that Stacey would have to live with him so he could help take care of her and the baby. Kevin said his son was the most beautiful baby he had ever seen.

Kevin walked over to his brother and pulled him aside to tell him about his plan to propose again to Stacey. Kevin told his brother that Stacey and his new son had brought so much satisfaction to his life and helped him become a better person and a stronger Christian. Eric jokingly told Kevin to wait until he started changing diapers and getting up in the middle of the night.

During the next couple of months, Kevin woke up at night to care for his son while Stacey rested. Kevin believed that he had to do everything for his child because it couldn't feed itself, change itself, and it certainly didn't ask to come into the world. As an adult, he wanted to do things with his child with joy. Stacey often told Kevin that she wished he was the father of her other son, because the real father was totally opposite from him. At work, Kevin already had his desk full of pictures of his son, and felt life couldn't get any better.

A year later, Kevin was enjoying his son, Jasper, who, just started saying daddy and was finally walking. Kevin said witnessing his son take his first steps and hearing him call him daddy was the greatest moment he had ever experienced. He was feeling good about his relationship and planning on having another child in the future. Stacey moved back home with her mother and had been acting a little uneasy. Kevin offered to hire a nanny to help Stacey during the day because he thought raising both kids alone might be wearing her out. She admitted to Kevin that Lamar had been trying to get back together with her.

She knew she could comfortably talk to Kevin about Lamar because Kevin had always been like a big brother to her and a willing listener to any of her problems. Stacey told Kevin that she couldn't believe Lamar didn't get her anything for Christmas. This shocked Kevin, especially since it was the first Christmas that he had spent with Stacey and his new son. Stacey even asked Kevin for his opinion on the matter. She asked if he thought Lamar was sincere about wanting her back. Kevin told Stacey, "I can't see why he wouldn't want something so precious back, but when a man mistreats and loses a jewel, and another man finds it, he may never again be able to have something as valuable again." Kevin went on to say, "I can't judge him, but if he loves you like I love you, his love is larger than life. Besides, there's nothing in the world I wouldn't do for you. You don't even have to sweat him about taking care of his son, because whatever the boys need, I've got." Kevin ended by saying, "Hopefully, Lamar will learn from his mistake and treat the next woman down the line better." Stacey told Kevin that Lamar had a lady that she hadn't seen her yet. Lamar told Stacey that his girlfriend's family reminded him of her family, and that she was very pretty. Stacey told Kevin that she wanted to see Lamar's new lady, but Kevin didn't understand why. She explained to him, "I just want to see what she looks like. For some reason, I always feel like I'm in competition with the ladies Lamar dates. I want to know I'm prettier, smarter, and a better dresser and I would do the same to you if we were to separate. I don't want to see him do better than me. That means I would have to come up."

A Man's Worst Nightmare

Over the next few weeks, Stacey grew very distant toward Kevin. She even left a message on his voice mail saying, "Kevin, I love you with all my heart. You have really been there for me, and I would never do anything to intentionally hurt you." Kevin was puzzled by the message. Her voice sounded as if she was about to leave the country. When Kevin called Stacey to talk, she didn't feel like it then. He asked her if she needed some extra space in the relationship, and she told him that she did. About two days later, Kevin received a certified letter from Stacey and enclosed was an envelope from the doctor's office. The envelope from the doctor was a DNA genetic test that proved Lamar was Jasper's father. The letter had instructions from Stacey saying not to contact her because she was going to be with Lamar.

Kevin broke out into tears as he read the letter and was totally distraught. Kevin tried to call Stacey, but his phone was blocked. Kevin's mom called and asked where Jasper was, and Kevin broke out into tears again. After Kevin told his mom the whole story, she told him that he couldn't get his money back, and to calm down and leave it in God's hands.

"To be honest, mom," he explained, "I ain't even trying to hear just pray about it, or anything about God. I'm gonna kill that bitch! I turned down a good job, and the bitch played with my emotions!" Kevin's mom tried to calm him down and told him that she was on her way over there. "Don't come over here," Kevin told his mother, "She has to pay!" Kevin's mom convinced him to calm down as she made her way to his apartment.

Kevin's mom went over and offered to cook his favorite meal. He said, "Thanks, but I'm really not hungry." Kevin's mom gave him a hug, and reassured him that he was a good man who just kept coming across the wrong women. She told him, "Don't worry, son. One day, when you aren't expecting it, God will send you someone who will be true to you." Kevin said sadly, "I just want to be by myself, live my life, and die an old man who never got married or had any children." Kevin's mom told him that wasn't what he really wanted, and that he was just upset. He told his mom that he did want that because making a relationship work was too hard and he was so tired of being disappointed. He went on to say, "Maybe I am just upset, but I can tell you one thing; never again will I have a lady that says she's mine. It's so much easier being the other man, because he already knows that the woman ain't no good for cheating on her man, and he knows not to fall in love with her."

Kevin said, "Besides, these women out here don't give you any respect unless you're dogging them out!" "That isn't true, Kevin" his mother replied, "There are women out there who will love you to death if you treat them like your queen." Kevin asked his mom why he hadn't met any of those women, and she told him, "You're probably just looking in the wrong places." "I don't go to certain places to meet women," Kevin told his mother, "I just approach women that I'm attracted to when I'm out and about." Kevin's mom told him, "Maybe you need to go to church to find someone to date." Kevin quickly replied, "Mom, the church ain't what it used to be. The same women you see in church are the same women you see the night before in the club." Kevin went on to say, "Besides, I go to church to serve God, and I don't want to be looking at women like Damn, she's fine. I want to get to know her." The only thing his mom could say was, "Don't do it then, baby."

Kevin said, "I'm going to be honest. If you see a woman in church with some nicely shaped hips and a nice backside, it's hard to walk up to them after church and say, "Hi, I'm Kevin and I'm looking for a Christian friend to get acquainted with and to share with in the Word. That may sound good but a brother's probably salivating at the mouth anticipating the sight of her in the nude, and that would be sinning in the house of the Lord." Kevin's mom told him, "Well, if you go around anticipating seeing ladies in their birthday suits, then you've got a problem." "Mom, I don't mean it like that," Kevin replied. "And sex isn't even all that important to me. It's just the fact that when you meet someone, the first thing that you are attracted to are physical features, and I don't want to feel like I'm perpetrating a fraud." Kevin's mom asked him what he was going to do. She even offered to let him move back home to be around loved ones for a while. "Mom, I'm so sick now, I need help. I'm going to a shrink to get some anti-depressants."

Kevin's mom advised him not to take any medication but to keep praying about it and the Lord would work it out. Kevin replied, "I knew you would just say to pray." Kevin's mom continued, "If the doctor recommends it, you might need anti-depressants. I just hate to see you on those things. It seems like they take all the life out of people." Kevin said, "No, they don't take the life out of people, people take the life out of people." Then Kevin's mother told him, "You have to stop putting your faith in man. Man will let you down every time." Kevin said, "Mom, I don't put my faith in man, I put my faith in my so-called child's mother, and what's wrong with that?" All Kevin's mom could say was that people are a trip. His mother then asked him if he would be okay. He told her he didn't have any other choice, and she decided to go ahead and leave. Kevin thanked his mom, as he hugged her, and walked her to the car.

At some point Stacey must have unblocked Kevin's telephone because he was finally able to reach her on the telephone. She told him she was sorry, but never to call her again. She also said that she would be with Lamar from then on and that he would be visiting her more frequently, and she didn't want to piss him off. Nevertheless, Kevin continued to call Stacey for about a week straight, and he finally received a letter in the mail from her. In the letter, Stacey told Kevin how she would leave his house and go straight to Lamar's house to have sex with him. She went on to explain how bad she felt for giving Kevin some of Lamar's pussy, and that looking at Lamar and Kevin was like looking at roses and dirt. Stacey also said that she hoped she ran across Kevin's fine ass brother so she could have sex with him. Stacey described how every time she was with Kevin, she felt like throwing up. She also wrote that she would never have a baby with someone as ugly as Kevin. He sat quietly and read the letter in disbelief, and couldn't face the fact that Stacey felt that way about him.

Kevin truly thought he and Stacey were both victimized in the past and that they loved each other too much and had been too close as friends to hurt each other like that. Stacey apparently didn't feel the same way. She ended her letter with, "Have a nice life, and by the way, no more phone calls, as you can see they won't be necessary." After reading that letter, Kevin decided to leave Stacey alone. He was in really bad shape at that time. Kevin had lost all his confidence and self-esteem. Everyone told Kevin that he shouldn't feel like a nothing, because if he was nothing, she wouldn't have invested her time in him. He told them that regardless, it hurt. He told everyone that the money he lost in the relationship was nothing and could be replaced, but the lost emotions, like believing he was a father for over a year, could never be replaced.

Male Commentary on "The Game"

Tony, Kevin, Steve, and Calvin were at Kevin's house having a man's-night-out barbecue. The most popular topic of discussion was the Black woman. Steve started off by saying how sisters of the 90's want to meet ready-made doctors, lawyers, million-aires, and athletes. "One reason men lie so much is because sisters won't give them the time of day if they're trying to get on their feet." He also said, "Sisters these days want you to be a financial genius or something, but yet they may not have anything to offer." He continued with, "I wonder if that's because so many sisters grow up in poverty and are afraid to go on struggling like their parents did. I can say one thing; marriages lasted a lot longer in our parents' generation than they do now. In addition to that, most rich men cheat because they think they're above the law. To get where you want to be financially takes a lot of hard work, and if sisters were willing to take chances on brothers with potential instead of looking for a Black Donald Trump, they would be better off." Kevin added that he was so tired of hearing about irresponsible Black men.

Kevin went on to say, "Every man in this room has dated a sister with a child. What about all the black men willing to accept sisters with children? Sisters want you to take care of them and their chil-dren. I see fewer white women with children out of wedlock. The numbers are very small regardless of what they do as far as abortion goes. I'm also tired of sisters who can't stand on their own two feet, yet think brothers were issued a money tree. Their attitude is that we're supposed to have money because we're men, but what about them? And it's also amazing to me how disrespectful our sisters are to us. For example, if you know something is wrong with your woman, they're quick to say "none of your business" when you ask questions. However, it is our business when they need money to pay a bill or something. They try to delegate what is our business and what isn't. In other words, they have a secret personal life that they won't let you into, but their financial lives you can know everything about so you can come out of your pocket."

Then Tony said, "Say players, peep this. You know how you hear about so many women wanting a companion, but when they get a guy who genuinely cares about them and wants to spend time with them, he's labeled worrisome. They say things like, 'Why do you always want to be up under me?' but when they have a guy who they might get to see once a week and he never returns their calls, they fall head over heels in love. They'll even dump a guy who's there for them all the time for some spontaneous foolishness. I'm also tired of sisters telling me they're such good Black women. If we're dating, show me don't tell me. They carry around a lot of mental and emotional baggage about things they did in their last relationship, and say, 'I'm not going to do that for another man again.' So in other words, they'll deprive you, the man helping to raise their kids and helping to fight her battles, because of some past experience with a loser. Don't deprive me of anything I can get somewhere else. I'm not taking less from anybody; and they wonder why brothers leave them so much. One thing about a lot of non-Black women is that they can say that their last man was an asshole and not hold you responsible for their past."

Kevin said, "Check this out. Have you ever seen sisters in business clothes or just out looking good? They won't even speak to a brother in passing, and if they do make eye contact, they're either rolling their eyes at you or looking at you like dirt. But let that same sister's car break down, and you'll see her break her neck to be nice so she can get a boost or something. It's amazing how pleasant they can be while you're working on their car. And don't let that same sister have brothers passing by while her hood is up. She calls them everything but a child of God. But, this was the same sister who played high society all week or walked around like she was better than everyone else." "That's real," Calvin said, "But why do women get mad when we hang out with the boys? The difference is, we can chip in and buy a twelve pack of beer, and have some chicken or grab a burger or something. I've noticed how women always say they don't eat fast food, but when you go to their house, all they have in the trash can is fast food bags. And you know if you're hanging out with your lady, the fist place she picks to eat is a seafood restaurant where her plate alone is going to be three to ten times more than what you would spend chillin' with the fellas. Then you have to worry about paying five dollars for every drink. Heck, it's more economical to hang out with the fellas. Hell, the tip alone is what you spend all night with the boys. Man, I usually pay three dollars at the most when we chip in for brew, so hanging out with the guys is just so much more economically feasible. Of course it's good to take your lady out on the town, but doing it too much during the course of the week is too much of a strain on the pocket. So hangin' with the boys is kind of a getaway. It's actually a good business move. How many women say, 'You've taken me to an expensive restaurant four times this week. That isn't good for your wallet." I mean think about it, most of the time when I go on a date, as soon as we get to our destination, she's asking me to pop the trunk so she can put her purse in there. So don't sweat me about going out unless you plan to treat some of the time."

Kevin went on to say, "What trips me out are holidays like Valentine's Day. Women think it's an additional birthday for them. What I mean is, if you and your lady wake up and you both say 'Happy Valentine's Day,' more than likely your girl will be pissed off if you don't have a romantic day planned with gifts and the whole nine yards. If you don't, your name is dirt with her and all of her friends. However, that same lady can't buy you anything or plan anything and she's still pissed at you. Isn't Valentine's Day a day of love? It's supposed to be a day that two people share and express their happiness towards one another. Why do women think Valentine's Day is their day to be spoiled? They put all the responsibility on the man and he's just supposed to be happy to do all this. I believe that's why so many brothers hate Valentine's Day because it becomes more of a chore for the guy and an extra birthday for the lady. Usually, all the brothers end up with in return is a dent in their savings account. Now don't get me wrong, there are some sisters out there going all out for their men on Valentine's Day from what I hear. Hey, but I never had one." The guys all responded back, "Me either!" Kevin continued, "It just seems like a lop-sided day and not a day of sharing. I'm also tired of women saying they don't have time for a broke-ass man or they can do badly by themselves. Hey, maybe two average incomes can make it under one roof with the right attitude to start with and good fiscal management skills. It is amazing how these women with no money, maybe very little education, and possibly children, feel that they deserve to be with eligible bachelors like Grant Hill and shit. They're always up in paid brother's faces and don't have anything to bring to the table. And brothers, we know that if we have some mediocre income job, it's still tough for us to get a pretty woman with nothing going for herself, but they seem to think that their sexuality is so much more powerful than ours is. Women seem to think, 'Hey, I got my hair, nails, and toes done, I have a new outfit on, a three hundred dollar purse, with twenty dollars to my name, and now I'm ready to go out and catch some athlete, doctor, or lawyer.' They just live in so much of a fairytale world. Don't get me wrong, I mean those guys get an erection just like the rest of us, but that doesn't mean she has a chance to be his wife. Another thing is, women truly feel that if they have sex with a man, they're giving up more. However, nowadays, women have sex just as much as we do, if not more. I mean, back in the day, women were a little more discrete with their bodies. I can say they may have been giving up more, then. Today, sex is no longer sacred, and they want it just as much as we do, and they get off to it just as much. So why do women still throw it up in your face that they're sleeping with you and all that? Hell I'm sleeping with her too. God didn't make your body parts any more special than mine. We were all created equal, so why do women try to act like they're giving more than we are? Well, players, let's eat. I'm tired of talking about this subject."

Later that week, Tony and Kevin hung out at Tony's house. Tony wondered if anyone he ever dated actually loved him. Tony questioned Kevin and asked him, "What makes a woman love you?" Kevin answered, "Tony, I don't know if a woman ever truly loved me. You see, we're nice guys. We do all the right things, say all the right words, and we fall into the category of being sweet." Kevin continued to say, "In the past, I would ask the women who said they loved me why they loved me. More often than not, I got answers like, 'You're sweet.' or 'You're a good provider.' or 'You're nice to me.' My thing is, those are things that you like about someone, or qualities that you admire in someone. However, anyone can be nice to you, or be a good provider, or be sweet, but love is much deeper than that. When I love a woman, I love the way she smells, I love the way she walks, I love the pitch of her voice, I love her sense of humor, I love the total make-up of the woman. I truly feel that there isn't another person on this earth that could be a carbon copy of her, but anyone can be nice and sweet."

Tony then asked, "So what is the strongest love relationship?"

Kevin told him, "That's easy, it's when a mother bonds and protects her baby. Most mothers are very over-protective of their children. If anything happens to her child, like the child being dropped or scratched, the mother cringes and can basically feel the pain of her baby. Sometimes, I wonder where that love goes. I mean, sure you become an adult, and you're capable of taking care of yourself if you get sick. But should it get to the point where when you call your mom and tell her you have the flu she tells you not to bring your germs to her house."

Tony told Kevin, "I don't think I'll ever get married."

"Why do you say that?" inquired Kevin. Tony replied, "Sometimes I just don't think there's anyone out there for me." He went on to say, "And it's sad because I don't require a lot, but it seems like everyone is in a relationship for self. Haven't you heard the saying, 'Don't be with who you love, be with who loves you,' and that's the attitude these people have out here."

Kevin finally said, "Man let me get out of here. You're depressing me." Tony said, "Alright man, I'll holler at you later."

Tony decided to spend the weekend at his brother's house. Tony's brother, Steve, was in the kitchen cooking T-bone steaks and sipping on a long-neck beer, while Tony sat in the living room drinking a cold beer and watched TV. Tony was sitting back watching videos, and a video by a young female group came on. The song had lyrics like 'What kind of car do you drive? How much money do you make?' and Tony shouted to Steve, "Man, look at what kind of world we live in. Listen to this song and what it's about, and it's in the Top 10! I think dating is like pros-titution these days, except the women are being their own pimps. These women don't care about a man's character or personality, they care about how fat his wallet is. The best prospect to a woman, is the man with the most money. I don't even think men are con-cerned with the way they look now, because they know that if they have deep pockets, they can get whatever woman they want. That's the bottom line. Good-looking men are not 'in' anymore, and neither is a good sense of humor. These women will take a man with the personality of a tomato if he has the cash. Think about it. They women expect a man to do 'X' amount of things for them financially, and in return, the man is rewarded sex. If a woman can't pay her bills, the first person she's going to run to is whoever she's sleeping with. They have an attitude like we owe them anyway." He went on to say, "Picture this: have you ever slept with your lady, and immediately after sex she says something like, 'Baby, I have to get this layaway out and I'm short about $60. Can you help me out?' and you give her the money.

Steve responded, "Hell yeah! And it makes me feel cheap, like a trick or something." "Well, Steve, what's the difference between that and prostitution?" Tony asked. Steve answered, "It's not too much of a difference. It's like you're just part of their regular clientele." "Thank you," Tony said.

Tony continued to say, "And what's so sad is, if you let a lady know you're in a financial crisis, you can count on being kicked to the curb. Oh yeah, they will ask you exactly what the problem is just so they can get deep enough into your business to find out if you're broke, so they will know not to mess with you anymorc."

Tony paused shortly, then said, "Think about this, too, Steve, we have more Black male thieves, drug dealers, hustlers, or whatever right now than we have ever had. And do you know what? If you talk to those guys, most of them do what they do to impress these women. When I was in school, I would ask some of my friends why they were in gangs, and they would all say the women love gangsters. And back then, that was the truth if you were in a popular gang. You could have any woman you wanted. You have to understand men are very female-motivated. Part of the reason I played sports was because I knew basketball players got a lot of play. Don't get me wrong, the cash is probably good to these guys, but they know the ladies wouldn't accept them if they were making nine dollars an hour. "I have to agree with the late Tupac Shakur, when he said, 'They say money brings bitches and bitches bring lies....' I would agree but money attracts all types of women, not just bitches. Women usually treat me like dirt until they see my car. Then I can't keep them out of my face. If they feel that you have some money, their perception of you completely changes. For example, you can date a woman who treats you like dirt and you would think she was evil and didn't know how to treat a man. However, you can take that same woman, let her date someone like Grant Hill, and that woman will appear to be the best woman that this planet has to offer. Do I deserve to be treated less than a man just because I'm not as successful as Grant Hill? Is he more of a man just because his bank account is larger? Realistically, I think if women became less materialistic and started accepting men for who they are, we would have fewer hustlers and less crime in the world. Tony said sarcastically, "What if women said, 'I'm attracted to a man that works eight hours a day and makes an honest living. I don't look for men who are financially able to take care of my spending habits and me.' I'm sure there would be more brothers doing the right thing. Think about it, drug dealers, these days, are dating educated women and women in the church, but they shouldn't be classified as Christians. Anyway

Steve, let me go to the store to get some beer, but think about what we were just discussing."

Tony called Kevin to find out what he was doing one evening. He asked Kevin what was going down, and Kevin told him he was just chillin' watching a movie and talking on the telephone. Kevin told Tony, "Do you realize at one point in the movie three of the women dated a married man?" Tony replied, "I don't get it. How can you complain about Black men, or men in general when you are just as guilty as they are? I could probably understand if those men lied and the women didn't know they were married, but that wasn't the case. How could you expect to get anything from anybody who is disobeying God? Isn't this movie supposed to be about positive, clean, wholesome sisters who can't find a righteous Black man? To tell you the truth, if you choose to mess around with a married person, you have sinned just like they have in the eyes of God." Kevin continued by saying, "Tony, watch the beginning of the movie. Sally went to a New Year's Eve Party, walked right in and sat down at a table full of couples, and said to herself that she was single, desperate, with no morals, and if one of those women turned her back, then she would take her man. Was the book or movie about the negative characteristics of Black men or the of Black women? Tony, to be honest, the only sister I felt sorry for was Brenda, because if she started off with nothing with that brother, helped him build a successful business, bore and raised his children, then he decided to leave her for a white woman. That brother was just a flat sell-out, and a poor excuse for a man. So anyway, what is going on with you, player?"

Tony said, "Shoot, nothing, just broke as hell." Kevin replied, "I heard that. I know how it gets between pay periods." Tony said, "Yeah, I think I will just stay in the house cause it's free. One of my lady friends asked me out tonight, but I told her I didn't feel like going anywhere. Because you know how it is these days when a lady asks you out, they still expect you to pay." Kevin said, "I know, and you can't tell them you're broke." Tony commented, "Please, I know not to do that. That's a sure-fire way never to see that lady again. Yeah, they'll still question your financial situation, as if they really care, but they're really trying to find out, is this brother really as broke as he says he is."

Kevin said, "What's so cold is that a woman has no problem telling you that they have three dollars in their purse and they don't get paid for another week. The reason is, they want us to say "Oh, I can give you some money," or they just don't care if you know they're broke, because they know we won't leave them because of that."

Tony said, "Those situations are so unfair because it seems we have extra pressure on us just because we are men. Women are quick to say, 'Tell me what's wrong, or why are you so quiet.' Most of the time, it's about our present financial situation, that we know we can't share with them. It's just the fact that we know what not to say, and that is that we are broke." Kevin then tells Tony, "Come on by, I will lend you some money. Think about it. I give all these women that come in and out of my life money that I never see again, so I'm sure I can lend one of my long-time friends some money. So come on by, I will be here."

Kevin had another Reyna flashback that day. He went to the gas station on his lunch break and ran across Larry's homeboy Cedric. Kevin never got too close to Cedric, and usually they barely spoke to one another. However, Cedric was all teeth when he saw him, and he actually tried to hold a conversation with Kevin, but Kevin gave him the old brush off. Kevin said Cedric had this look like Larry had been bragging to him about taking his lady. He did hear that Larry had been bragging about the whole situation. Kevin let Larry get to him once when he heard him bragging, but Kevin called Larry about a month after their encounter and apologized for tapping on his windshield and then told Larry that he just lost his temper because he still had feelings for Reyna. Larry then apologized and Kevin wished Larry and Reyna the best. He told Larry that he wasn't a player-hater. About a month after the conversation with Larry, Kevin was at a get-together with a bunch of mutual friends and one particular lady told Kevin, "Larry said you called him and apologized like you didn't want him to beat your ass." The lady then said that Larry told her that Kevin was acting like a little bitch on the telephone and was basically giving him permission to fuck his lady. Kevin couldn't believe what he was hearing. He was so pissed off that he wanted to go to Larry's job to confront him but he didn't want to give Reyna the satisfaction of having two men fight over her. The lady told Kevin not to sweat it and that Reyna was not worth going to jail for. Kevin left the party and started thinking back about the last picnic that Reyna had attended. It was about three months ago; Reyna's car was being serviced over the weekend. She was at Kevin's house, when Michelle called and reminded her of their barbecue. Reyna said that she would get Kevin to drop her off at Michelle's house after he took her son to her mother's house or agreed to baby-sit until the barbecue was over. Reyna asked Kevin to use his car but he told her he had some running around to do. Kevin dropped the baby off and took Reyna to Michelle's house where all the ladies were waiting for her. He asked Reyna why were they outside waiting, and she told him they were having their barbecue at the park. He asked if he could come along, but Reyna told him no because it was a woman thing. Kevin thought to himself that they were overdressed for an outdoor barbecue. They almost looked like three hookers. He went back to his side of town to take care of some business, and later got a call in the middle of the night from Reyna, who asked him to come to pick her up so that she could go pick up her baby and go home. Kevin realized as he was reflecting that he remembered that Reyna had told him about the weekend that she had met the other guy she dated. It was the same weekend that he took her to Michelle's house for a barbe-

cue, and Reyna told Kevin she met the guy at a barbecue. Apparently, Reyna went to a barbecue that
wasn't just a woman thing. Kevin couldn't help but
think that Reyna had actually asked him to use his car
to go. Kevin thought to himself, that was another time
he hand-delivered Reyna to another man.

Kevin was also angry with Reyna's friends. He
would cook for them, had birthday parties for Lil'
Jason, and all her friends would come by with their
kids. Kevin would also let her friends come by to
shower and dress before they went to the clubs. He
gave them rides to wherever they wanted to go, and
on their birthday, he would buy them something really nice. He looked back and thought about how they
were in on it the whole time, and probably encour-
aged it. He told the lady that memories of Reyna
brought back a lot of pain, and it continued because
he was still finding out about a lot of things that he
had overlooked when he and Reyna were together.
Kevin said, "I really don't think I can go through another relationship like that again." The lady told Kevin,
"You're a good man. Reyna was just an unapprecia-
tive bitch." Kevin told her, "Thanks. I really needed to
hear that."

One night, Kevin and his NBA friend Calvin
decided to follow each other in their cars and go
around town macking for telephone numbers. Kevin
and Calvin pulled up at the mall, close to the mall's
movie theater. Kevin saw this tall cutie dressed in
white and tried his luck. He introduced himself and
the woman introduces herself as Nicole. Kevin and

Nicole immediately hit it off. She walked Kevin to his car so they could exchange phone numbers, and Nicole told him that he was driving her dream car. Meanwhile, Calvin went inside his Lexus sports utility to get a drink of Gatorade. Nicole noticed and asked Kevin if that was his friend's car. Kevin told her yes, and she said, "You guys must be rich!" Kevin told her, that they do all right. Nicole asked Kevin and Calvin to walk her over to the movies because she was going back inside. They asked who she was with, and she said, "I'm with two ladies and my sister." Kevin replied, "Well, I'm hanging out with my friends tonight. Why don't you guys come over to my place and join us?" Nicole told him that the ladies wanted to go to the club afterwards, and she asked him what time would be good to stop by. Kevin replied, "I don't care, come on over after the club." Nicole said that was fine and Kevin told her to just give him a call.

Kevin and Calvin went back to Kevin's house where they were discussed meeting Nicole. Kevin asked, "Why would young ladies come to see some niggas' they don't even know this late at night? I was just kind of flirting, not expecting them to bite back." Calvin said, "Well, I think she was just pulling your leg anyway."

Kevin's phone rang about 11 p.m. and it was Nicole. He asked, "What's up?" and Nicole told him that the other ladies didn't want to come after the club. Kevin asked if she was on a mobile phone, and she said she was on a pay phone because her sister kicked her out of the car for wanting to come see him.

Kevin asked where she was and she told him she was a couple of streets away from his house. Kevin told her to give him directions so he could come get her. Kevin asked Calvin to ride with him because it sounded kind of spooky. Kevin saw Nicole talking to a guy in a white Camaro so he stopped about thirty feet away because she seemed to know the guy. Nicole walked up to Kevin's car and got in. He asked Nicole who was talking to in the white Camaro and she said, "Just a guy who said it was too late for me to be standing here by myself, so he wanted to stay until you came to get me." Kevin told her that was cool.

Kevin pulled in his driveway with Calvin and Nicole, and when they got into the house, he offered her a drink, which she graciously accepted. Kevin sat a distance from Nicole because he didn't want her to feel uncomfortable, besides, Kevin hadn't planned to try anything anyway.

Kevin heard a knock at the door, and it was a short guy in a local restaurant outfit asking Kevin if Tracey was there. Kevin told the guy that he had the wrong house. He went back to tell Calvin and Nicole what happened and described what the guy looked like and what restaurant he worked for. Calvin asked Kevin what he told the guy, and Kevin jokingly said that he and Tracey were busy having sex. The guy stopped by after Nicole had been there for ten minutes and Kevin looked outside and told Calvin and Nicole that the guy was still out there. The dude finally left after about ten more minutes, and Nicole asked to use the telephone. Nicole said she was paging her sister. She kept the telephone in her lap, and when it rang again, she answered it, which Kevin thought was very rude. Nicole said her sister was at the corner, and Kevin asked, "Why doesn't she just come to the house?" Nicole told Kevin that her sister didn't believe in turning down streets she wasn't familiar with. Kevin said, "Well, let me get my shoes so I can drive you down to the corner." Nicole had already walked out of the house with Calvin and began walking to the corner. Kevin got in his car and saw a Chevy Blazer with the guy that had knocked on his door in it while Nicole was visiting. Kevin flashed his bright lights on them, and Calvin jumped in Kevin's car. Kevin asked what happened, and Calvin told him that the guy yelled 'Sis' and Nicole said that was her brother. Calvin said, "I kept my hand on my crouch like I had a gun to make sure he didn't try anything." Kevin said, "I don't understand. I described the guy, his outfit, and where he worked to Nicole, and she said nothing." Calvin replied, "That's because she and the guy were trying to set us up. Nicole probably wanted to see if you had a lot of expensive merchandise in your house, and thank God you don't." "Fuck you," Kevin told Calvin, "I have heard of women trying to set up men these days. For instance, a woman meets a man at the club who has a Rolex, a nice car, and he is pulling out hundreds every time he buys a drink. Then, the woman goes home with the guy or takes him to a motel so she can get him naked. That's when the ladies friends break in, hold the guy up, and take everything he has from his jewelry to his car. They tie the dude up and make their getaway. Usually the lady wears a wig and contact lenses and gives a fake name. That means the brother is just shit out of luck!" Kevin concluded by saying, "Well, Cal, I'm not going out to meet any of those scandalous bitches for a while."

Depression

I'm depressed, and I don't know why.
I have my health and strength,
but I'm still not satisfied.
When I lay down,
I toss and turn,
hoping to come up with answers,
but my soul just burns.
I can't take it,
I want to inhale,
take a deep breath,
And my problems exhale.
When I take a deep breath,
they don't go away,
same old problems,
day after day.

CHAPTER VI

Nose wide open...

Steve was in the mall picking up a couple of items when he noticed a woman passing out surveys. This woman was a model for a woman's department store. He couldn't believe his eyes. She had skin that looked as smooth as a freshly bathed baby's. She didn't have one blemish in her face or any part of her body that was exposed. This woman had long black curly hair, and teeth as white as chalk. As he stood there staring intensely at this goddess, Steve was trying to come up with something to say to her. The mere essence of her beauty had left him speechless. He began to just follow her and stare at her in awe. If there were such a thing as somebody wanting to drink a person's bath water, he would be the poster man in this situation. The young lady finally turned around and asked Steve if he was following her. Steve looked at her with his sad puppy dog eyes and nodded his head up and down. She smiled and said, "Hi, I'm Lena." Steve introduced himself as well. His palms were sweaty and he was so nervous that Lena thought that it was cute and teased him about it. She kind of dominated the conversation and asked him for his telephone number. Steve couldn't believe his good fortune. He had always told himself that a woman that beautiful would never call him. He thought that she was just trying to be nice. Steve was sort of dating a young lady in his complex named Mary, but they weren't serious or anything. Mary had a boyfriend but would stop by and visit Steve from time to time. Steve and Mary weren't intimate, she just had a lot of problems with her man and some financial problems as well. He was always available for her when she wanted to talk. Mary was beginning to really like Steve, but she just had too many problems for him.

The following day after Steve met Lena, he was at home watching videos with Mary. His phone rang and the moment that he picked up the phone, he had that feeling that it was someone new. He asked who was calling, and the sweetest voice he ever heard, replied, "This is Lena." He just quivered knowing that it was Lena on the other line. Lena almost immediately sensed that he had company. She asked him if he had company and he said "No", while walking towards his room so that he could close the door. He later admitted to having company and Lena said, "Well I didn't know that you were seeing someone, so I will let you go". Steve immediately informed her that the company was just a friend. Lena said that she was calling to invite him to a barbecue but she could see that he was pre-occupied. He then asked if he could get her telephone number. Lena said, "No, because you didn't tell me you were seeing someone". He asked her to please call him later because he really wanted to talk to her. Lena told him that she would think about it. He asked her to please give him a chance to explain later and that the situation wasn't what she thought. Lena simply said, "Good-bye Steve."

Meanwhile, he heard his front door close and rushed out to see Mary getting into her car. He apologized to her and Mary said, "Oh, you know that it's cool like that with us." but Steve could see that Mary was hurt by the incident. Lena called the next day and she and Steve talked for about three hours. He explained to Lena what the situation was with Mary and told her that it wouldn't happen again if she gave him a chance to get to know her. Lena replied, "We're getting to know each other now."

Steve and Lena began to talk every night for about two weeks. They started going out on dates twice a week. During their third week of dating, Lena asked Steve for one hundred dollars and he gave it to her without a problem. She had a daughter named Mesa, but Lena didn't want Steve to meet her. Shortly thereafter, Lena called Steve and asked him to buy her an outfit for her to wear out of town. He told her it wasn't in his budget. Steve didn't hear from Lena for a couple of days.

The following weekend, Steve took Lena to a family fish fry. He was the highlight of the dinner. After the dinner, everyone from his brother to his grandmother called him to tell him how pretty Lena was. Lena was not only the prettiest woman he had ever dated, but she was also the prettiest woman that any man in his family had ever dated.

The very next weekend, Steve took Lena to another get together and his friends told him how beautiful she was. One of his friends even made the comment that "You can't keep a lady like that man, she's just too much woman for you." Steve started to feel an obligation to keep dating Lena because of the peer pressure from his friends and family. She wasn't affectionate towards Steve, in fact she wouldn't even let him kiss her. Steve and Lena would have had a lot of fun when they went out, if only Lena wouldn't always bring up the subject of getting money from him. She would constantly ask Steve for money and he would give her what he could afford. He had begun to get stressed out behind her and the money issue. Lena called Steve and asked him to get her a beach house for the weekend and he said, "Sure, that would be a nice get-a-way for us." Lena replied, "It isn't for us, it's for me." She said, "I'm going to prob-ably have to find a babysitter for Mesa because I'm so stressed my doctor told me that I need a get-a-way weekend." He told Lena that he didn't know if he could do something like that. Lena said, "Just go ahead and make the reservations and I will call you later." Later on that day, he received a page from Lena and she asked if he had made the reservations. Steve replied, "I didn't have that much available on my credit card." Lena furiously said, "Goodbye and don't you ever call me again." For the next several weeks, he would page her and wouldn't get a return call. She would screen his calls on her caller ID at home. He finally decided to drive by her house to get her address so that he could send her a letter. He wrote a desperate, begging letter, stating that he would give her all of his extra money and would do anything he could to make her happy. He also instructed her to put a special code in his pager when she called, with the year being '99. He said that that would signify the year that they would get married.

With all my heart to my Bride-to-be...

Steve finally received a page with the year '99 as a code just a couple of days after he had mailed his letter to Lena. Steve and Lena began to date again and she did indeed take most of Steve's extra money. He gave her so much of his money, that he was privately thinking about filing bankruptcy. Lena still wouldn't even give him a kiss. At the end of every date, she would ask him for a hug and stick her cheek out for Steve to kiss it. Even though she was not affectionate towards him, he still ran behind her and would do anything for her. In spite of not knowing her intimately, they started making wedding plans. He took her to the bridal store and paid an arm and leg for a wedding dress. He had begun to give her half of his paycheck to help pay for the wedding. Steve bought Lena the two-carat, princess-cut, diamond ring that she had picked out. He was ready to spend the rest of his life with her because Lena, despite her intimate shortcomings, was very fun to be with when she wasn't trying to get money from him. He wasn't really that disappointed that they had not been intimate because he wasn't sexually motivated.

On the same night that Steve gave Lena her ring, a strange thing happened. When Steve tried to call Lena, her telephone had been disconnected. He tried paging her but didn't receive a return call. It wasn't until a couple of days later, that Lena dropped the bomb on Steve. She told him that she was about to get married to someone else and for him not to page her anymore. He asked Lena how long she had been dating the guy. She replied, "I've known him about three months longer than I've known you." He said "Baby please don't go through with it. I want to marry you. I'm the only man for you." She said that it was too late and that they were getting married the next weekend. Steve asked if he had helped to finance her wedding. Lena chuckled a little as she replied, "A little bit." Then he asked, "Is the wedding going to have the same color scheme as our wedding was supposed to have?" Lena replied, "Yeah."

Two months later, Steve called Tony to say that he couldn't sleep. When Tony asked why, Steve burst out into tears says "I'm supposed to get married today." Tony stayed up and talked to Steve all night. Steve would also cry a lot while driving because the song that was supposed to be played during his wedding ceremony was a top ten hit and it was often played on the radio. He would change the radio station because he said that he couldn't bear to hear slow songs anymore. He was totally distraught and heart-broken indeed. He knew it would take him sometime to get over this one.

Family War Wounds

Kevin decided to visit his uncle Freddy over the weekend. His uncle was going through a divorce. Freddy's wife, Rosie had become friends with a guy named Brian at work. Brian and Rosie would go to lunch together and discuss problems that each of them was having in their relationships. It was a very innocent friendship. Brian wouldn't flirt with Rosie, but he would compliment her style of dress, her cooking, and her hair. That was more than Uncle Fred would do. Fred had began to take Rosie for granted which wasn't good because Rosie was the type of woman that needed her man's attention. Fred was a big sports fan, and once he got in front of that TV and a game was on, he didn't want to be bothered. He was also an athlete, scout and the official "couch-coach" in his own mind. Needless to say, when the game was on, the rest of the world around him was off. He truly did love Rosie with all his heart, it's just that sports was his first love. It always had been and always would be. Fred used to be known as the six-month man because none of his relationships lasted more than six months. It was very difficult for a woman to get close to Fred, because he was a "wanna be jock." Not only that, he wouldn't spend much time pursuing women because he would rather watch a game on TV. It was damn near impossible to get Fred to miss a good game, but when he met Rosie, he made unusual sacrifices. He began to set the VCR to record his games so that he and Rosie could go out.

At forty-five years old, Fred still claimed that he could lace his sneakers up and go with the best of them on the hardwood. He had however, limited his activities to coaching a little league basketball team. Aunt Rosie was tired of hearing about guys that Fred said didn't know NBA defense instead of hearing how beautiful she looked or how wonderful her dinners were. Rosie felt neglected and longed for the compliments and attention that she so craved and used to receive from Fred. Eventually, Rosie and Brian began to spend more and more time together. Fred didn't mind at all because he saw it as an opportunity for him to watch his games in peace.

One evening, Rosie and Brian decided to go to happy hour together and they laughed and drank all night long. They had more fun together that night than they both had experienced in quite a long time. They danced to nearly every song that came on, slow ones as well as fast ones. The last time Rosie had danced and laughed so much was the time she and Fred partied on the beach in Jamaica on their honeymoon. Rosie and Brian decided to sit in a booth when Rosie confessed to Brian how unattractive Fred made her feel. Brian reassured Rosie that she was a very attractive woman and that Fred was a very lucky man to have her. Rosie's eyes suddenly began to fill with tears. Brian gently picked up one of her hands, looked her straight in her eyes and said, "You have absolutely no reason to feel undesirable." Rosie started to feel a little dizzy. She didn't know if it was the alcohol or the ambiance from being there with Brian. All she knew was that she hadn't felt that way since she was a teenager in high school. Brian slowly leaned over towards Rosie's face while staring intensely into her eyes and kissed her on the lips. Acting on impulse, Rosie returned his passionate kiss and they indulged themselves for several minutes. Afterwards, Rosie admitted to Brian that she had been attracted to him for quite some time. Brian couldn't believe that they had both felt the same way and neither of them had ever let on until that night. They decided to go back to Rosie's house for a while before Fred got home from work. Rosie and Brian were all over each other before they could get inside of the house good. Leaving a trail of clothes, under-wear and socks, the couple headed straight toward the bedroom where they began to make passionate love. Suddenly they heard someone banging on the door. Rosie jumped out of bed, ran and looked through the peephole and discovered that it was Fred. Rosie had dead-bolted the door, something she never did especially knowing that Fred hadn't made it home yet. Fred immediately sensed that something was going on so he shattered the living room window with his baseball bat and entered the house. He pro-ceeded to follow Rosie to the bedroom where Brian was fumbling with his coat. Fred began to approach Brian with the baseball bat and in a panic, Brian pulled out a thirty-eight from his coat pocket and shot Fred in the chest. Rosie hysterically ran to the tele-phone and dialed 911 for help. Several minutes later an ambulance arrived along with a police car. Rosie ran outside practically naked and begged the police, "Please don't take Brian, it was an accident. He is innocent." Uncle Fred was rushed to the hospital and had to have major surgery to remove the bullet from his chest, but he lived. Fred was released from the hospital one week later and found him-self home alone.

While Fred was home recuperating, the phone rang and he answered it. It was Rosie's mother who lived out of town calling to check on her. Rosie was not at home at the time and Fred proceeded to tell her mother what had happened two weeks prior. Rosie found out about their conversation and became very angry and vindictive. Rosie scratched up Fred's car, slashed all four of his tires, and threw a brick through his car window. Rosie harassed Fred so much at work that he lost his job. She also withdrew all the money from their joint bank account, even though the majority of the money had been deposited by Fred.

Rosie and Brian are now together, and poor Uncle Fred has not been the same since. Fred hasn't been on a date in ten years and has no intentions of dating anytime soon. Maybe in time Fred will learn to trust again, but now he is just another victim.

The Reprisal of Reyna

Kevin had a reason to be excited again. He had saved several thousand dollars and was about to buy his dream home. He finally caught up with his delinquent debts and would have no problem getting approved for a house. Kevin's dream house was a two-story home with a pool in the backyard, just like he always wanted. He was on his way to see the loan officer to close the deal. The loan officer came out to greet him and said, "Everything looks fine on your credit, except for the repossession of the car." Kevin replied, " I still have my car, I don't have a repossession on my credit report." The loan officer handed Kevin a copy of his credit report and he saw the car that he had co-signed for Reyna on his credit report as a repossession. "Unbelievable," he said. Reyna owed only four more car payments that totaled twelve hundred dollars and she let them repossess the car. He couldn't believe it. A relationship that was several years old was still coming back to haunt him. He explained to loan officer, "Look, I co-signed for an ex-girlfriend several years ago and on the application, she put that I was her husband. Of course we were not married, but at the time it was okay with me because we were planning to get married." The loan officer replied, "Let me go talk to my boss and see what he says." He came back into his office, closed his door and walked right up to Kevin. "You have two options. One, you can pay the twelve hundred dollars, or two, get your ex-girl friend to sign an affidavit and have it notarized stating that you were not her husband at the time." Kevin agreed, however he didn't have a clue as to what to do. He didn't have an extra twelve hundred dollars, and he had too much pride to pay twelve hundred dollars on a past mistake. He talked it over with some close friends and every one of them advised him to call Reyna.

He decided to go ahead and call Reyna, but first he said to himself that he had to have a couple of drinks. He also told himself that he would feel more comfortable talking with Reyna if he had a buzz just in case she still possessed some type of spell over him. When he called Reyna she answered the telephone and immediately recognized his voice. She asked him what he wanted in a joking way. He explained to her what he needed for her to do based on the information he received regarding his credit report. She said, "Oh you can only call me when you need something." He responded, "Yeah, we don't have anything left to talk about." She told Kevin that she missed him and so did her son, Jason. Kevin replied, "Yeah, I really miss Jason too." Reyna replied, "And you know that you really miss me too." Kevin told her that he did not miss her. Reyna took it to another level by telling him that she wanted to have dinner with him and talk about some things. Kevin bravely declined. Reyna told him that he was her Pooh, and that she had been telling everybody how much she missed him. Then Reyna said, "If I sign the affidavit, will you let me move into your new house?" He responded, "Hell No! You're no good for me." She asked Kevin to come over to her house to give her a kiss. He asked, "What for?" She replied, "Because I miss your kissable lips." He told her that he has no feelings for her anymore and to be very honest, he hated her. Reyna responded, "Don't be a player-hater because I took some change out of your pocket." By this time, Kevin was getting a little irritated and asked her if she was going to sign the affidavit or not. Her reply was, "Not! Especially if it isn't going to benefit me in some way." Kevin decided to try another approach. He figured in order to get what he needed from Reyna, he was going to have to talk the only language a woman like her understood. He offered Reyna three hundred dollars to sign the paper. She responded by making a counter offer of five hundred dollars. When Kevin told her that he didn't have five hundred dollars, she replied, "Oh well." He then decided to get off the telephone with her and just wait a while before he tried once more to purchase his home. Once again his dream had been killed temporarily by his past mistakes.

He thought to himself how you really don't know a person when you first get involved with them. As Kevin sat out on the balcony of his one bedroom apartment, he began to reminisce on how he treated that tramp Reyna like a queen. He thought about what his Uncle Fred had told him, "You can't make a whore into a housewife." He couldn't believe that he once cherished someone who was nothing more than a money hungry con-artist. He couldn't believe that this was actually the woman he had once wanted for his bride. Woman like Reyna gave decent hard working sisters a bad name. He now understood why so many brothers and friends of his, treated some women the way they did. He knew brothers that would have just made Reyna their personal whore and just used her for sex. He wondered why he had to fall in love with her. He thought back about how many thousands of dollars he had invested into that whop-sided relationship and how much time, labor, and love went toward the wrong woman. Damn, he'd put blood, sweat, and tears into trying to make her happy, and now after all this time, he was still paying for it. He used to actually question God as to why he was punishing him by allowing him to love Reyna. He eventually realized that the whole experience made him self-reflect and discover that he had forgotten to love himself first. How could he love or expect someone to return the love that he deserved unless he loved himself first. It also made him a stronger person in a lot of ways and helped him to deal with defeat better. Kevin now worked harder to prove to the world that he is somebody and someone worth loving. He is now so focused on fulfilling his own needs and pursuing his own dreams that he sometimes feels as if he's possessed and nothing or no one can get in his way.

Going to new Places, Same 'ole Faces

Kevin left the bar to go to the restroom and when he returned to his stool, Reyna was standing right next to him. She tried to hug him but he pushed her away. She said, "Hello honey, I've missed you, aren't you going to buy me a drink?" Kevin responded "Hell No." Reyna smiled at him and tried to pinch his cheek, but he knocked her hand back. She knew that she had once hurt Kevin, and she tried to rub it in his face every chance that she got   Reyna said, "Kevin you know I could have you back if I wanted you. You have been cursed. You're in love with me." Kevin said, "I don't have any feelings for you, and even though hate is an emotion I've never felt for anyone, you are about to make history." Reyna replied, "Take that back!" Kevin of course, said no. She told Kevin that he was always so cute when he got angry. Kevin replied, "Whatever" and left the club. It was clear that Reyna would haunt him for a long time to come.

A week later, the boys were all hanging out at Kevin's house watching a basketball game. Kevin suddenly got up from the couch and turned off the TV. He turned to the room full of black men and said "You know what?" The guys were all kind of puzzled as they looked at one another. Kevin continued, "We as black people don't love each other." Tony responded, "Break that down my brother." Kevin said, "Black people are always talking about the white man and how they treat us so bad. Peep this. Look at us. We have all been played for money by our sisters. They have cheated on us and have damn near destroyed each one of us. Look at our brothers! They rape our Black woman, they lie, steal and cheat on our sisters. To make matters worse, some brothers are physically and mentally abusive to our Black women." He went on to say, "I don't know about y'all, but the white man has never hurt me as much as my own Black sisters have hurt me. We do the things that white people did to us as slaves, but we don't even see it. How can you expect another race to love and respect you when we can't even love and respect each other?" Tony replied, "You know what, you're right. One of our biggest problems is just being honest with each other. If you find someone else to love, why not just admit it? Why do we need more than one partner? Other races have already labeled us as being animalistic! Why are we so greedy? Personally, I don't believe the majority of our race place a value on Sex anymore. Sex should be sacred, not something you're doing just to get satisfied. We are supposed to be Kings and Queens, and making love should be something special. Look at the popular phrase our race uses when we are referring to sex." People like to use the term "Booty Call." How could something that had once been thought of as being so sacred now be minimized to the term "Booty Call?" Steve stated that what bothered him the most was that our people aren't very remorseful. "We will deliberately hurt each other carrying out these twisted little tricks or games just to be able to brag to our peers that we got over on somebody." Think about it, the only time a man or woman apologizes for something they did to hurt one another is when they have an ulterior motive. The individual usually wants to get back with the other person so that they can probably end up hurting them again. How many apologies have you received from someone in the past either by mail, phone or face to face? You usually don't, unless they're trying to get back in your life. Other than that, if they have no more interest in you, you usually never get an apology, no matter what they did to you." At this point, Kevin stood back up and replied, "We have to pay for all our decisions. We also can't put God on with our Sunday clothes and take him off when we get undressed from church. How many people are truly dating the way God would like for us to date? Not me, and probably none of you in this room, and definitely none of the people that we have dated. I'm challenging each one of you today, to put your trust in God and to love your brothers and sisters."

DO I TRY AGAIN?...

That is the question.
I tried before and learned a valuable lesson.
I learned that people can deceive you,
such as tell you that they will never leave you.
That sounds good, but if that was so,
I wouldn't be alone today looking out of my window.
Oh God! What could it be?
Do you have a bigger plan for me?
Oh c'mon. I've experienced plenty of heartbreaks.
When will it stop? I can't take this much longer.
Is this what life's about?
I've tried to understand, but maybe it's me.
I know I have a lot of love to offer,
but nobody cares.
When I try to share it, they act as if I'm not their's.
Oh man . . .Boy am I blue.
Every time I like somebody, they like somebody too.
But that's not what they tell me.
They wait 'till I'm in love,
then tell me it's somebody
else that they are thinking of.
Oh friend, What should I do?
Should I try again...
Or just feel blue?

EPILOGUE

The intent of this book is not to offend the many positive Black sisters who play a dual parenting role in bringing up our Black children. It is only meant to give a wake-up call to those sisters who intentionally take advantage of the brothers that are sincere about making a relationship work. It is also intended to give credit to a lot of positive God-fearing brothers that are out there and seem to go unnoticed. I have talked with many Black men as I have traveled through life who desire to get married and raise a family but often run into some of the same problems that many Black women do, infidelity, greediness, selfishness, lack of commitment, etc.

I do want my sisters to know that we are in this together and through Christ and self-enhancement, we can come out of this game we play with one another and live in harmony.